"Julie, what devil sent you across my path?"

His mouth descended, his kiss deepening as he parted her lips. He arched her toward him as one hand slipped beneath her lacy top.

"Adam—no—stop it at once." Julie's voice seemed strangled as she struggled to remove his hand.

He stared at her searchingly. "Perhaps you want me to stop because you'd rather I was someone else?"

"What are you talking about?" she managed to ask.

Who is he?" he rasped. "This fellow you imagine you're kissing—what's his name?"

"There isn't anyone—not now," she whispered. "*There isn't anyone.*"

"And I'm telling you I don't believe you. You're lying again, just as you did when I asked your name. And I refuse to act as a stand-in for anyone!"

Miriam MacGregor began writing under the tutoring of a renowned military historian, and produced articles, books—fiction and nonfiction—concerning New Zealand's pioneer days, as well as plays for a local drama club. In 1984 she received an award for her contribution to New Zealand's literary field. She now writes romance novels exclusively and derives great pleasure from offering readers escape from everyday life. She and her husband live on a sheep-and-cattle station near the small town of Waipawa.

Books by Miriam MacGregor

HARLEQUIN ROMANCE

2710—BOSS OF BRIGHTLANDS
2733—SPRING AT SEVENOAKS
2794—CALL OF THE MOUNTAIN
2823—WINTER AT WHITECLIFFS
2849—STAIRWAY TO DESTINY

Don't miss any of our special offers. Write to us at the following address for information on our newest releases.

Harlequin Reader Service
901 Fuhrmann Blvd., P.O. Box 1397, Buffalo, NY 14240
Canadian address: P.O. Box 603,
Fort Erie, Ont. L2A 5X3

The Malvern Man

Miriam MacGregor

Harlequin Books

TORONTO • NEW YORK • LONDON
AMSTERDAM • PARIS • SYDNEY • HAMBURG
STOCKHOLM • ATHENS • TOKYO • MILAN

Original hardcover edition published in 1986
by Mills & Boon Limited

ISBN 0-373-17004-1

Harlequin Romance first edition December 1987

Printed in U.S.A.

CHAPTER ONE

JULIE crouched on the bed and read the letter for the third time. The apologetic words, seen through a haze of tears, were now registering in her mind. Ross could do this to her? Ross—and Anna, her own sister? It seemed incredible.

Her mother came into the room. 'I thought I heard the mailcar go past——' She stood still, staring at the dejected figure of Julie huddled against the pillows. 'What on earth is the matter?'

'This came from Ross,' Julie said in a dull flat voice as she handed her mother the sheet of paper. 'He and Anna——' Further words failed her as her grey eyes brimmed and the tears rolled down her cheeks.

Claire Forsyth read the letter, then sighed. 'My dear, these things are apt to happen. I'm afraid it's a situation you'll just have to accept. If his preference leans towards Anna there's little you can do about it.'

Julie's eyes flashed with anger. 'When did he decide that he preferred Anna, may I ask? He's made it very clear that *I* was his preference. When did he change his mind—and why?'

Her mother sighed again. 'I've no idea. However, I *do* know I have two daughters and I want you both to be happy. This appears to be Anna's turn.'

Julie's eyes narrowed thoughtfully. 'I've been dumb. I should've guessed there was something in the wind. Haven't you noticed the trouble she's been taking with her appearance lately? Her hair's no longer lank and she's been using much more make-up.'

'Yes—I've noticed. The eye shadow and mascara certainly make a difference to her, whereas you need to do next to nothing to make yourself look like somebody out of a magazine.'

Julie ignored the compliment. 'She's deliberately set herself out to catch Ross—to steal him from me,' she declared angrily.

'But—he wasn't yours to steal,' Claire reminded her in gentle tones. 'You weren't engaged—at least, not officially.'

'Mother—you know perfectly well I *expected* to become engaged—and now *this*. Can't you see? The mere fact that he's written to tell me about Anna and himself proves he feels guilty about *me*. And that's another thing. Why couldn't he face me? Why did he have to take the cowardly way out by just writing a letter——?' Her words were interrupted by the shrill ringing of the telephone. 'If that's Ross I won't speak to him,' she declared vehemently.

As her mother left the room she crumpled the letter into a tight ball, threw it across the room then lay back to stare at the ceiling. It was now more than two years since Ross Mitchell had taken over the neighbouring property, she realised; then, musing, she recalled that from the beginning his arrival had meant a difference in the lives of Anna and herself.

Before he'd loomed on their horizon they'd known few young men near their own ages, and those brave enough to come speeding along the drive on high-powered motorcycles were soon told by their father that his daughters did not go gadding about the countryside on those hellish machines.

But one day when Ross had called to see if he could buy some hay from Father, Mother had seen the wisdom of inviting the apparently eligible new neighbour to Sunday tea. After that it hadn't been long before he'd become like one of the family.

It meant that she and Anna no longer lacked for partners at the parties held in other country homes, at dances in the nearby Ashhurst township, or at functions in the city of Palmerston North which was only about twelve miles away. Ross usually found a friend who made up the foursome, and he collected the girls in his new English Rover, a vehicle of which Father heartily approved.

Granted, there'd been times, particularly recently, when he'd partnered Anna instead of herself, Julie realised, but this had occurred when he'd been so slow in asking her she'd found it necessary to accept other offers. And although she wasn't happy with these arrangements she felt she was being wise in letting him know he wasn't the only stone on the riverbank.

Her mother returned to the room. 'That was Ross on the phone,' she admitted. 'He wants to talk to Father about becoming engaged to Anna. I've invited him to have evening meal with us.'

Julie was aghast. 'You mean—*tonight*?'

'Yes. You'll have to face each other sooner or later and it's better to get it over and be done with it. By the way—where is Anna? Didn't I see her in her jodhpurs?'

'She's out walking Big Boy. It's my guess she knew I'd get this letter today so she's keeping well away until she thinks I've simmered down. She knows she must only walk Big Boy—but I'll bet she's having a darned good gallop out of sheer excitement.'

Claire Forsyth's maternal instinct was stirred. 'Julie dear, I know this has been a shock, but I don't want you to spoil Anna's happiness. You'd be wise to have a good weep to wash it out of your system, then bathe your eyes in cold water and get yourself under control. You must face them both this evening, otherwise they'll think you're running away.'

Julie sat up and stared at her mother. 'Run away? Yes—that's exactly what I'd like to do. I want to get right away from the pair of them. I don't want to see them holding hands and laughing into each other's eyes. I'm telling you, mother—*I can't stand it*.' She sank back

against the pillows as a sob almost choked her and the
tears flowed afresh.

'That's right—cry it out,' Claire advised. 'Get rid of it
and then you'll be able to hold up your head and let
Ross see he hasn't broken your heart.' She left the room
quietly.

As the weeping spasm passed Julie began to think of
the situation with Ross. For the last six months she'd
been waiting for him to ask her to marry him. She felt
sure she was in love with him because she was so happy
when they were together. They liked the same things,
they laughed a great deal and he danced so well. Life
was fun when she went out with Ross.

There was also the fact that, by marrying Ross, she
could stay close to home. The thought of moving away
from home when she married had always been a tiny
nightmare in the back of Julie's mind, but when she
became his wife she'd be only a few fields away. The
thought had sent a glow of contentment through her
entire being.

But apart from these reasons for becoming Mrs Ross
Mitchell people were now *expecting* them to marry.
When is your engagement to be announced, dear? her
aunts living in Palmerston North were apt to inquire.
And with much less tact her cousins were inclined to
comment with a slight laugh, *What—no ring yet?* Even
their friends and acquaintances had them firmly linked
together, and she was well aware of the glances flashed
at her left hand without a word being said.

In actual fact Julie had expected her engagement to
Ross to be announced on her twenty-first birthday.
There had been a large party in their home and she'd
been showered with gifts of all types except the one for
which she yearned—an engagement ring. But Ross had
said nothing.

Despite the casual kisses he'd been in the habit of
giving her he allowed the event to pass without a word
of love in her ear, or the slightest mention of their

future together. For her the party became something of an anticlimax, but she told herself she must understand he was not yet ready for commitment and that she must exercise patience.

In the meantime, and without her being aware of it, Anna had also had her eyes upon Ross. Although only a year her junior Anna had always seemed to be much younger than herself—except that recently she appeared to have become more grown up. It was almost as though she had matured sufficiently to make a sudden leap from the teenager state into womanhood.

By the time Ross arrived that evening Julie had steeled herself to accept the situation. She steadfastly avoided his glance, yet forced herself to observe him from a more objective point of view. He was beginning to look like a real New Zealand farmer and slightly older than his twenty-seven years, she thought. The sun had given his complexion an outdoor ruggedness and had bleached his light brown hair to a paler shade, even turning it blond in parts. Given another year's sun it would almost match her own honey-gold tresses.

At last he drew her aside. 'You received my letter?'

She met his pale eyes squarely. 'Do you mean that rambling scrawl telling me you've fallen in love with Anna and hoping we'll always be friends?'

'I'm sorry, Julie——'

Pride came to her rescue. 'Sorry for what?' she snapped.

'For—for not making up my mind before this.'

'And you've done that at last?'

'Yes—my decision's been made. I hope you'll understand.'

'Perfectly. It's good to see a man with a mind of his own—small as it is.' Her lip curled as she glared at him with the utmost contempt. Then, appalled by the intensity of her own anger, she wondered if the love she'd had for him was already turning to hatred.

During the meal she knew that her mother cast

flashes of anxiety in her direction, and that Anna's flushed face betrayed an inner excitement. However, most of the conversation was dominated by her father as he droned on about his colt's latest win at the races. Father adored Big Boy, or so it seemed.

'There he was, right at the back,' Walter Forsyth exclaimed, his grey eyes alight with pride. 'And then he made his run. He mowed them down leaving the rest of the field for dead—and this included Gallant owned by that Malvern fellow on the other side of the Gorge. Ha! Pipped at the post. he was. The upstart!'

Claire frowned at her husband. 'In all fairness I don't think you can call Adam Malvern an upstart, dear, After all, his family took up land at Woodville when the place was being cut out of the bush over a hundred years ago.'

Walter eyed her coolly. He leaned forward, tapping the table with a stiff forefinger. 'As far as I'm concerned any man who steals my trainer is an upstart. And there was Molly, too. She's your cousin, don't forget. She should've persuaded Ted to stay.

Claire laughed. 'For heaven's sake be reasonable, Walter. She's Ted's wife. She *had* to go with him.'

'She shouldn't have married him in the first place,' Walter snapped testily. 'She could've done better for herself. The idea of my wife's cousin marrying my horse trainer——'

'You were pleased enough at the time,' Claire retorted dryly. 'You decided it was a situation that would keep them both here for life—Ted watching over your horses, Molly at my beck and call.' She paused to send an apologetic glance towards Ross Mitchell. 'Please forgive us—this must be boring for you.'

He'd been listening with a half-smile playing about his lips, a glint of amusement in his light eyes. 'Not at all,' he returned politely. 'It's something that occurred before I came to the district and, without wishing to sound unduly curious, I'd be interested to know what happened.'

Claire smiled but shook her head. 'We won't go into the details of it now because it'd upset Walter—and that's not what we want at the moment, is it?'

'Definitely not.' Ross sent a grin towards Anna.

But the mood Julie was in did not allow her to let the matter rest. Leaning forward she spoke to her father. 'In all fairness to Ted—and if I remember correctly—it was you who gave him the sack. You'd had a quarrel over a jockey. But although you'd dismissed Ted you didn't expect him to leave. You thought he'd get as far as the corner of the main road near Ashhurst, then come crawling back, cap in hand. You were sure he'd ask to have his job back again.'

'But it didn't happen that way,' Anna chimed in. 'When he reached the corner he discovered a man in trouble with his horse-trailer. He had a flat tyre and two horses on board, so of course Ted stopped and helped him—and that's how he met the Malvern man. That upstart, as you call him, Father, could see that Ted was used to handling thoroughbreds, and as he happened to be looking for a new trainer at that particular time the rest followed naturally. He gave Ted a job.' Anna paused for breath, her cheeks slightly flushed.

'Molly says Mr Malvern's been very good to them,' Claire put in calmly, her blue eyes holding a touch of defiance.

Walter flashed a suspicious look towards the end of the table. 'You've been to Woodville to see her? You've visited the Malvern stables? I'd have thought that as my wife——'

'Don't be silly, Walter. Of course we haven't been to see them, but we've spoken to Molly on the phone several times.'

'But I'd *like* to meet him,' Anna said artlessly. 'Molly says that Mr Malvern is the most handsome and the

most eligible man in the whole district.' She flashed a
teasing look towards Ross.

'Is he indeed?' Walter cut in. 'No doubt he's also
conceited, overbearing and somewhat arrogant in his
behaviour towards women. My oath—it was good to
see Big Boy put that hack Gallant in his place.'

'If you don't mind, I think it's time we changed the
subject,' Claire said a little wearily. 'Anna dear—pass
your father the salad oil—it might help to soothe his
ruffled mood.'

'My mood is not ruffled,' Walter declared, irritated.
'It's perfectly calm—as always.' He turned to Ross.
'Now then, young man, I understand that you and
Anna want to become engaged. Well—I can't see
anything to stand in the way of it, although I must
admit I thought it was Julie you had your eye on——'

A tense silence followed his words. Ross stared at his
plate while Anna sent Julie a smile of thinly veiled
triumph.

For the rest of the evening Julie sat in a daze as the
voices went on and on around her, Mother's
predominating. How long did they intend to be
engaged? Wedding plans must be prepared well ahead.
She must begin to make a list, and if Ross would give
her the names of his friends and relatives he wished her
to invite—oh yes—she must make inquiries in
Palmerston North about the best caterers——.

The discussion continued with questions darting across
the room until Julie became obsessed with a strong desire
to scream. If only she could rush outside and catch Big
Boy, leap on his bare back and ride at a mad speed over
the fields. Instead she dug her nails into the palms of
her hands and took numerous deep breaths.

Later, as they were preparing for bed, Anna's face
beamed as she said, 'I'm so happy—I can hardly believe
it's happened. It was all so sudden.'

Despite her own misery Julie was curious. 'Oh?
When—exactly—did it happen?'

'It was at that last dance we went to. You'd made arrangements to go with Robert what's-his-name—so Ross took me. During the evening we were dancing a slow waltz. The lights had been dimmed and he was holding me very close to him. I looked up at him just as he looked down into my face—and suddenly we both *knew*. It was a glorious moment—like finding something we'd both been searching for. He's taking me to Palmy tomorrow to buy a ring. Would you like to come with us?'

Julie almost choked as she said, 'No thank you. Traipsing about Palmerston North always makes me tired.'

Anna's face showed disappointment. 'Please come— I'd like you to be there to help me choose.'

Julie kept a grip on her temper. 'For Pete's sake, Anna—how can you be so stupidly naive? I'm the last person Ross would want breathing over his shoulder while he buys a ring for—for *you*.'

'Oh—well—perhaps you're right. But we'll have to go together quite soon to see about the material for my bridal gown. There's a lovely shop on Broadway—and of course you'll be my bridesmaid. I'd like you to be dressed in airy-fairy floating tulle or nylon in different shades of greens—or perhaps mauves——'

'We'll see about that later,' Julie snapped crossly.

'Aren't I lucky you're so good at sewing,' Anna went on guilelessly. 'I'm so glad Mother persuaded you to take that dressmaking course, because it's really given you the expert's touch.'

Julie was startled. 'Are you suggesting that I'll make your wedding gown?'

'Of course. Why not? You make things so easily——'

'You've got to be joking.' Julie's voice was cold. This was adding insult to injury. Further, she'd had enough for one day. Emotionally she was thoroughly worn out, She felt *drained*.

It was a relief to lie in her bed, and as she stared

wide-eyed into the darkness she was hit by the full impact of the situation. It meant that what she had imagined to be love on Ross's part had been nothing more than brotherly friendship, and while he'd been taking her out he'd been waiting for her younger sister to reach the state of realising she loved him. Again the tears trickling down her cheeks soaked into the pillow until at last she drifted off into a restless sleep.

The next morning she woke with a feeling of heavy depression bearing down upon her and, for several minutes, she lay gazing at the ceiling until the cause registered in her mind. It brought a nasty jar and she knew she had to become used to the idea of Anna being engaged to Ross. Not only become used to it, but learn how to cope with it, and this, she knew, would be difficult.

She would have to face the aunts who'd questioned her so often about her association with Ross—and the jeering cousins who'd looked for a ring. They'd see a ring, all right, but it wouldn't be on *her* finger. It'd be on Anna's. And there were so many other friends to be faced. She turned to the wall and wondered how she could do it. Even the thought of going to the Ashhurst shops gave her the horrors because everyone in the small town knew her—and Anna—and Ross, of course.

If only she could creep away and hide in some place where she was not well known. A job in Palmerston North, perhaps? But what could she do? She was untrained for anything apart from being able to sew well and help Mother in the house.

Three years ago she'd been keen to study veterinary science at Massey University on the edge of Palmerston North, but that plan had coincided with the upset between her father and Ted Lewis; then, when Ted and Molly had left, Father had demanded Julie's presence at home to help her mother run the household. In any case he didn't want a daughter of his taking up veterinary work. There was always the risk of being kicked by a horse or by a mad cow, he'd declared.

Julie had missed Molly who, as Mother's youngest cousin, had been more like an older sister to Anna and herself. Molly had come to live with them when her parents had died in a motoring accident and had become like an extra hand for Mother. Even after marrying Ted and moving into his cottage she had returned daily to vacuum, dust, bake and put clothes through the washing-machine.

Yet despite the odd phone calls Julie hadn't seen Molly since the day she'd departed with Ted, and suddenly she had an urgent desire to fling herself against the plump motherly figure. Molly would understand her misery. She could talk to her about it and get it all off her chest. And perhaps Woodville was where she could hide until everyone became used to the idea of Ross being engaged to Anna instead of to herself.

The mere thought of getting out of the house and away from Anna's constant chatter about her trousseau and wedding plans was enough to lift her spirits. She sprang from the bed, showered and dressed, but said nothing of her own plans until Father had left the breakfast table and Ross had called to take Anna to Palmerston North. Then, as the grey Rover disappeared down the drive, she went to the phone.

Molly was delighted by her request for a short visit. She did not ask questions and Julie made no explanation. There'd be time enough for that later. A few clothes were thrown into a bag and she told her mother she was going to Woodville.

'I quite understand, dear,' Claire said gently. 'I know you've had a shock, but don't worry—you'll get over it.'

Julie smiled wanly. 'That's what you think, Mother. I suppose Father will be hopping mad with me because I'm going to Molly and Ted.'

'You leave him to me. I'll tell him you're doing one of your periodic rounds of friends and relations. I won't tell him you're going only as far as the first step.' Claire paused to regard Julie thoughtfully. 'I think you're doing the right thing by going away for a while. I wouldn't like your—your disappointment to become obvious enough to spoil Anna's happiness. Fresh fields will be good for you. They'll enable you to view the situation from a distance and they'll give you something different to think about.'

'Something other than myself, you mean, Mother?'

'I didn't say that—nor did I mean it. Give my love to Molly—and watch out for the handsome Mr Malvern.'

'Huh! *Him!* I'll not be interested in him. I'm finished with all men—utterly and completely.'

'For the time being,' Claire Forsyth smiled.

A short time later Julie drove along the highway in her small red Fiat which had been a twenty-first-birthday present from her parents. Thoughts of Ross sprang about in her head as fury, rather than self-pity, caused her to grip the wheel until her knuckles whitened. *'How dare he place me in this embarrassing position?'* she gritted aloud as she made a determined effort to push the image of his face from her mind.

Soon the steep walls of the Manawatu Gorge loomed before her and care was now necessary while driving along the four-mile shelf of road which twisted and turned above the rushing waters of the narrow river. The ravine divided the Ruahine and Tararua mountain ranges, their bush and scrub-covered slopes rising steeply on either side.

Beyond the Gorge the small township of Woodville lay surrounded by peaceful farmlands, and from its short main street, it was easy to follow Molly's directions to the Malvern stables with their white-railed fences and the large horseshoe attached to one of the entrance pillars.

A white weatherboard house was situated a short

distance along the drive, and beyond it Julie could see
the white painted walls of the stables and sheds. She
drove to the back of the house and parked near a long
veranda which had several small rooms opening from it,
and as she left the car to walk past them she caught a
glimpse of Ted bending over a person who lay on a bed.
Was somebody ill? she wondered.

Molly, as plump as ever, welcomed her with open
arms but asked no questions. She led Julie to a guest-
room and showed her the bathroom. 'I'm about to
serve lunch,' she said. 'Come back to the kitchen when
you're ready. Ted'll be in soon.'

Julie took only moments to tidy herself by raking a
comb through the honey-gold hair that fell about her
shoulders, and when she returned to the kitchen Ted
was already in the room. He was a sturdily built man
who had handled horses all his life, and he now
embraced Julie with genuine affection.

'It's good to see you, lass. I'll say it's high time you
came to pay us a visit.'

Molly swept a critical glance over his furrowed brow.
'How's young Tim? I thought he was walking very
stiffly.'

Ted sighed. 'And with good reason. He's developed a
nasty boil on his backside. It's right where he sits. He
did pacework for me this morning, but he's asked to be
excused from further riding during the next few days. It
puts me in an awkward spot.'

Julie looked from Molly to Ted. 'Who is Tim?'

'He's our apprentice jockey,' Ted explained. 'I was
hoping he'd walk the filly for an hour this afternoon.
She's racing next week, so it's imperative to keep her fit.
I've got other work lined up so I'll have to find
somebody else.'

'Would it be possible for me to help?' Julie asked.
'You know I can ride.'

Ted's face cleared. 'I sure do. Didn't I teach you
myself?'

'But suppose Mr Malvern sees her?' Molly demurred anxiously.

'Well—suppose he does? So what?' Ted demanded.

'You know he's allergic to females riding his thoroughbreds. He won't allow any of the aspiring girl jockeys near them.'

Ted's lined face became even more wrinkled as he grinned. 'I'll tell him Julie's different. You'll see—it'll be okay.'

When lunch was over she changed into a pair of fawn jodhpurs and a green jersey which threw its colour into her eyes. Ted led her out to the stables where a grey filly stood waiting, and having legged her up into the saddle he adjusted the stirrups and gave instructions.

'Her name's Cloud. Take her for a couple of miles along the road until you see a wide white farm gate. Don't trot—don't canter—just let her have a nice walk. If she wants to stop and nibble don't allow it. Keep her going. Got it?'

Julie nodded. 'I understand. I used to do it for you at home—remember?' She sighed. Those times seemed so long ago.

He nodded. 'Of course I remember.' Then, as though unwilling to talk about those earlier days, he went on, 'You'll find she's been beautifully mouthed and has a lovely disposition. She'll give you no trouble at all. Off you go——' He patted the grey rump.

The quiet country road, lying about four miles from the main highway and its traffic, was ideal for walking a thoroughbred. Cloud behaved perfectly, stepping daintily to follow the grassy verge while Julie gazed at the flat surrounding farmlands bordered by the foothills of the Ruahine ranges rising on her left. She hadn't thought of Ross since her arrival, she realised with a sense of satisfaction, but now his face began to loom before her. However the image was short-lived because before it could assert itself it was wiped away by the sight of a man on horseback who cantered towards her from the opposite direction.

He drew rein a short distance ahead on the other side of the road, and she knew that he watched her approach; then, as she drew near, she found herself gazing into a face that had a hard mouth, and dark eyes that glared at her from beneath black brows.

'Who the hell are you?' he demanded curtly and without preamble.

Her chin rose as she stared back at him. 'I can't see that my identity is any concern of yours.'

'You can't? Then let me ask you another question. What the devil are you doing on my filly?'

His filly? The words gave her a shock. This must be none other than the formidable Adam Malvern, although forbidding was a more suitable description, she decided as, for some reason unknown to herself, she became conscious of an inner quaking. Then, pulling herself together she told herself she was being stupid. Why should she be afraid of this person? He couldn't possibly affect her—even if he was this Malvern man she'd heard about.

He raised his voice. 'Are you deaf? I asked you——'

'I heard you,' she cut in. 'There's no need to shout. You'll frighten the horses.' She ran admiring eyes over his black gelding, judging it to be about sixteen hands.

'You're not very smart at answering a simple question,' he rasped impatiently.

She regarded him thoughtfully. As Father had indicated, he was arrogant. No doubt he expected everyone—especially women—to jump to his commands. Well—he needn't expect to find her grovelling at his feet. She'd stand up to him.

'Surely the answer's obvious,' she said at last. 'I'm walking Cloud for Ted. Did you think I was stealing her? When I steal a horse I usually gallop away at high speed. I don't walk sedately otherwise one is liable to be caught.'

'Very funny,' he snapped. 'Who are you?'

She looked away evasively, having no wish to identify herself to this man who was obviously annoyed by the mere sight of her riding his filly. Her name would be sure to register with him, causing him to connect her with the owner of Big Boy, winner of the recent race in which his own Gallant had been beaten—and if she wished to stay for a period with Ted and Molly she'd be wise to avoid any disruption that knowledge of her identity could bring to them.

However, she knew she had to say something. 'My name's Julie,' she told him briefly.

'Is that all? Just—Julie? Most people admit to a surname of some sort unless they're ashamed of it, or have something to hide.' His voice had become cold.

'My name's Julie Sterling,' she admitted after a pause. It wasn't a lie, she assured herself, because her full name was Juliet Sterling Forsyth. She'd been given her mother's maiden name, a fact for which Molly could vouch, and even Molly herself had been a Sterling before her marriage to Ted. 'I'm staying with Molly and Ted for a few days,' she added.

He appeared to be satisfied. 'Where's Tim?' he demanded.

'He's—er—indisposed. He asked to be excused from riding this afternoon. Now do you mind if I keep moving? This scintillating conversation with you isn't giving Cloud her walk, Mr Malvern.'

He wheeled his horse and crossed the road to her side. 'I'll accompany you,' he informed her icily. 'Cloud is a valuable filly. I don't like to see her in the unprofessional hands of a stranger, especially when she's due to race next week.'

'Thank you for the lack of confidence,' she retorted angrily. 'Do you think Ted would've put me up on her if he hadn't been aware of my riding capabilities?'

'Knows them well, does he?' The words were drawled mockingly.

'Of course he does. Didn't he—teach me to ride? I've known him for a long time. Molly's a distant relative.'

'Oh.' The answer seemed to satisfy him to the point of accepting her presence without further veiled belligerence.

They rode abreast and she kept her gaze steadfastly ahead, refusing to allow her eyes to stray towards the man at her side. As Molly had said, he was handsome in a rakish sort of way, his dark blue polo-neck jersey doing nothing to disguise his breadth of shoulder, his fitting jodhpurs hugging long muscled legs that indicated he was tall.

His deep voice broke the silence between them. 'You said Tim's indisposed. What's the matter with him?'

'He's—he's got a boil where it hurts to sit.'

'Only the one?' His tone was sharp.

'You're very unfeeling for the poor boy, Mr Malvern. Surely one's enough—or do you consider he should be ignoring it?'

'Not at all. On the contrary I'm concerned about him, Miss Sterling. Or does that surprise you?'

She was startled by his use of the name. The deception sent the colour rushing to her cheeks but she felt it wiser to say nothing. Instead she listened to his explanation.

'Where there's one boil there are usually several to follow. Unfortunately apprentice boys and even full-blown jockeys are prone to them. Their constant fight is against gaining weight, therefore they don't eat sufficient nourishing food and their blood becomes poor. Boils come as a result.'

She was well aware of this fact but had no intention of displaying her knowledge although she nodded with understanding. 'It's a tough life when the boys are denied all the things they like such as hot pies, sweets, fish and chips—especially fish and chips.'

He gave a light laugh, then went on affably, 'Ted told me that weight was his problem. In his younger days he wanted to be a jockey but turned to horse training because he became too heavy. Most trainers are ex-jockeys.'

'You've known him for a long time, Mr Malvern?' The question came artlessly, really for the sake of finding something to say. At the same time she realised it was a stupid query because she knew exactly when and how this man had met Ted—and she also knew it furthered the deception concerning her own identity.

He said, 'I met him quite by chance about three years ago. He'd been working for a self-satisfied individual who was idiotic enough to give him the sack over something that was really a trifle.'

Anger caused her to draw a sharp breath. *Idiotic— self-satisfied*——. He was speaking of her father whom she was unable to defend, yet she knew there was much truth in the accusation. Her father, she felt, had been most unwise over the affair with Ted.

'Ted's a good reliable trainer,' Adam Malvern went on. 'I've been more than satisfied with his work. Forsyth was a fool to let him go, but no doubt he's a man with a closed mind, one who refuses to listen to explanations.'

Julie bit her lip and remained silent. Basically an honest person, she felt the mantle of hypocrisy wrapping itself about her shoulders. She longed to admit that she was Juliet Sterling Forsyth, but feared that the admission would earn her his contempt.

Strangely, the thought of his contempt filled her with dismay although the reason for this was something she was unable to define. She was in a state of hating all men—wasn't she? Her recent experience with Ross had taught her that not one male was to be trusted out of sight—hadn't it? So why should she care a tuppenny damn for this—this Adam Malvern's opinion of her?

It just didn't make sense.

CHAPTER TWO

THEY rode in silence for several minutes until curiosity forced Julie to say, 'Do you know what caused the quarrel between Ted and his—his former employer?' Why her father's anger had been so intense was something she had never understood, and it would be interesting to learn Mr Malvern's version of the event.

He gave a slight shrug. 'I know only what Ted told me. I believe it happened at a race meeting. The jockey Ted had engaged to ride Forsyth's horse had been injured in an earlier race. He'd had a fall and had departed in the ambulance. When Ted went into the jockeys' room to find a replacement there were only a few boys available—one of them being the son of an old friend who had recently died.'

'That's right—I remember,' Julie said unguardedly.

'You do——?' The dark eyes swept a rapid glance over her.

'I remember Molly saying something about it.' She explained hastily, staring straight ahead.

'Then you'll probably know that the boy pleaded for a ride, and although Ted knew he hadn't the experience of the others he gave him the opportunity.'

'Ted's always been very kind-hearted,' Julie said warmly.

'This time he was too kind-hearted. The horse didn't have a chance because the boy allowed it to become pocketed in the mob and he was then unable to get out for his run on the straight. Forsyth couldn't understand why Ted had chosen this particular boy, and when he knew that sympathy had been at the back of it—it'd been the last straw. Forsyth had ranted and raved about the many costs involved in getting a horse as far

23

as the starting gates—and Ted had been sent down the road.'

Memory of the unfortunate incident now loomed clearly in Julie's mind. She and Anna had shed copious tears while Mother had dissolved into a fit of weeping as Molly had begun packing their belongings. Father had stormed with fury, while Ted had remained white and silent until he and Molly had driven away.

Adam Malvern drew rein, his commanding voice cutting into her recollections. 'This is as far as we'll go. Turn her round and we'll head back to the stables.'

'But I haven't taken her the full distance,' Julie protested. 'Ted said I was to take her as far as a wide white farm gate. I think I can see it in the distance——'

'And I'm telling you this is sufficient,' he snapped, his jaw tightening as irritation crept into his voice.

'Ted has given me my instructions and I intend to carry them out,' she retorted stubbornly. At the same time she sent him a bright smile which was intended to lighten the situation as they continued towards the distant gate. Watching his face from the corner of her eye she could see that his mouth was still tight, and for several moments she almost expected his hand to shoot out and grab the rein to turn Cloud's head towards home.

Instead, to her surprise, he glanced up and nodded towards Whariti Peak situated near the southern end of the Ruahines. Even from her own home on the other side of the range the high mast of the television relay station placed on it could usually be seen pointing skyward like an accusing finger, but now it had become shrouded by the mists of heavy clouds.

'Whariti's wearing one of his darkest cloaks,' he remarked in a warning tone. 'I also know that deep blue tinge the ranges take on just before rain. I trust you won't mind getting drenched because we could be in for an October cloudburst.'

Julie had come out unprepared for rain, and now, as

she glanced up at the heights she knew a sudden uneasiness; however, pride kept her moving forward. 'It won't be much,' she said hopefully but without much conviction. 'I suppose—being near the mountains you're prone to sudden showers.'

'Sudden downpours would be a better description. Haven't you noticed the extensive areas of buttercup?'

She smiled. 'Do they also mean rain?'

'They mean wet land that needs tile draining and dressing with lime to rid it of sourness.' His tone had become terse.

'Yet they look so beautiful. They're like huge golden carpets.'

They rode in silence until they reached the gate, but just as they were about to turn the horses their faces were splashed by large drops of rain. He pointed to a pine-sheltered barn in the field. 'We'll go in there and shelter until it blows over. There's no sense in getting wet.'

She frowned as he leaned down from his horse to open the gate. 'Won't we be trespassing?' she asked uncertainly.

'Not exactly. I happen to own this land.'

'Are you telling me the Malvern stables stretch to this distance?' she queried as she followed him through the gate.

'Not at all. The Malvern stables and the Malvern farm are two separate properties. The stables have a small block of good land suitable for grazing the horses in work, while the farm consists of undulating hill country which drains well and doesn't become too wet. You won't find it golden with buttercups,' he added.

They followed the farm track from the gate to the barn where they stood watching the falling rain. At least Adam Malvern appeared to watch the rain, or perhaps he was examining the black Aberdeen Angus cattle that had moved at their approach before dropping their polled heads to continue grazing.

But Julie found her interest lying in neither the pastures nor the cattle. Instead she covertly examined the man beside her. As she'd imagined he was tall, her own head coming only as high as his shoulder. There was an athletic agility about his movements, she noticed, and she was also acutely aware of the man's personal magnetism. A handsome devil, Molly had said on the phone.

He turned his head and met her gaze, then ran dark eyes over her honey-blonde hair and petite form. 'There's not much of you, is there? You're little more than a child—probably still a teenager. You're about eighteen, I suppose?'

'I'm twenty-one,' she snapped indignantly.

'Really? So old? It's time you found yourself a man— or perhaps you've already done so.'

He'd touched a raw spot. Her face flamed as she retorted angrily, 'I'm not interested in men, Mr Malvern, nor am I likely to be for a long time.'

He sent her a sharp glance. 'Such vehemence. What would cause that attitude, I wonder?'

'Nothing at all,' she lied. 'I just don't like men— especially the tall handsome ones who consider themselves to be the salt of the earth and God's gift to the female population.' She allowed her eyes to glide slowly from his head to his feet.

'Is that a fact?' He gave a short laugh. 'There's reason for everything, Miss Sterling——'

Movement from several of the cattle caught his attention and she followed his gaze to where a chestnut horse cantered across the field towards them. As it drew near Julie could see that the rider was a woman who was older than herself and perhaps a year younger than Adam Malvern. She wore a light rainproof cape around her shoulders, and over it her long thick black hair, dampened by the rain, streamed down her back.

As she drew rein her hazel eyes swept Julie with a long stare before speaking to Adam. Smiling at him she said, 'I was on the rise when I saw you take shelter in the barn.' Then, as though unable to withhold the accusation, she said with a hint of reproach, 'You've been avoiding me all day, Adam. You weren't in for breakfast and we didn't see you at lunch time.'

'I've been busy,' he informed her coolly.

'So it seems. I think you owe me an explanation.'

The black brows shot up. 'I do? For what?'

She paused, glared at Julie, then ignored her presence as she said, 'Have you forgotten you were taking me to dinner at the Lindauer last night? I was dressed and ready at seven o'clock—but where were you? There wasn't a sign of you. Nor did Lucy have any idea of your whereabouts. At last I wondered if I'd made a mistake and that we'd arranged to meet at the Lindauer, so I got my Mini out and drove there——'

He frowned. 'You did——?'

'But did you turn up? No—you did not. I waited and waited until I was fed up with all those old Maori portraits staring at me from the walls. The girl kept asking me if I wanted to order, and I had to keep saying no until I felt a real fool.' Pausing for breath she glared again at Julie. 'I suppose you were with *her*—whoever she is.'

He made the introduction. 'Julie Sterling—Elaine Brady.' Then, looking up at the girl on the horse he said, 'Didn't you realise I was busy with Fay last night? She decided it would be a good time to have her pups, and this put the thought of any dinner appointment right out of my head. In short—I forgot.'

Elaine flushed. 'Are you saying you stood me up for a *dog*?'

'A bitch, actually. It's the bitches that give birth. I became worried about her because she appeared to be having a spot of bother. I spent the evening rushing about in search of a vet.'

'I notice you haven't even the grace to say you're sorry,' Elaine flung at him, her anger now evident.

He gave a small shrug but remained silent.

Julie sent Elaine a look of appeal. 'I think Mr Malvern expects you to understand the situation,' she pointed out.

'Do you indeed?' She favoured Julie with a long probing stare before her eyes narrowed slightly. 'Haven't we met before?'

Julie shook her head. 'I don't think so. If we have I'm afraid I've forgotten—although I don't see how I could forget you.'

Elaine looked gratified. 'Perhaps I'm mistaken, yet I feel sure I've seen you somewhere. Do you live in Woodville?'

'No.'

'Then—where *do* you live?'

'I'm—I'm staying with Ted and Molly Lewis.'

'But your home—where's your *home*?' Elaine persisted.

Julie's heart skipped a beat. Blast this girl and her curiosity. She glanced at Adam and became aware that although his eyes were on Whariti's distant peak he listened with interest. At last she found the words. 'My home is through the Gorge—near Ashhurst.'

'Ashhurst?' Elaine glanced at Adam. 'Isn't that where Ted and Molly were before they came to you?'

He nodded without speaking.

Elaine's eyes flashed back to Julie. 'Do you happen to know the Forsyths who live near Ashhurst?'

Julie returned her stare defiantly. 'Yes—I know them——'

'You wouldn't happen to be one of them—by any chance?'

'Yes—I happen to be Julie Forsyth.'

Adam swung round to face her. 'You *lied* to me?' he rasped.

'No. My name is Juliet Sterling Forsyth.'

'Why didn't you admit to the Forsyth part when I asked your name a short time ago?' Coldness now covered his face like an icy mask while his mouth formed a thin line as he glared at her.

She faced him defiantly. 'Because I didn't like your attitude—nor do I give my name to every stranger I meet.'

A light laughed came from Elaine. 'You've certainly blotted your copybook. He hates to be told a lie. A liar is as bad as a thief, he always maintains. Never again will he believe a word you say.' Satisfaction flashed across her face.

'Shut up, Elaine,' Adam snarled.

Julie shrugged as she looked up at Elaine. 'It doesn't matter because I doubt that I'll be seeing him again, therefore he's welcome to any opinion of me he likes to cook up in his own mind.'

She faltered slightly over the last words because they were so untrue. It *did* matter, and the knowledge that Adam would remember her only with bitterness and as a deceiving liar was like a sudden wound from a knife. Nor did she bother to ask herself why the opinion of this man, who she'd only just met, should matter so much. She just knew that it did.

Elaine gave a sudden shrill laugh. 'Sorry if I've tossed a dirty big spanner into the works.' She jerked the reins, causing the chestnut to cease cropping the grass, and the next moment the turf was being pounded as she galloped away.

As they stood watching the horse and rider disappear beyond the contour of rising ground Julie's mind switched to the cause of the broken appointment. 'Did you find the vet? Is Fay all right?' she asked sending him a sidelong glance.

'Yes—to both questions. She's now a contented mother with four pups, all doing well.'

His expression softened and she knew she'd struck the right note, one that would divert his mind from her recent deception. Pressing home the vantage she said, 'What does she look like? I suppose she's black and white like so many sheep dogs.'

'No—she's a long-haired golden-brown with a good head and eyes that almost speak when they look up at one. She has the ability to control a mob of sheep without instructions from anyone, and she's always mated with a top-class heading dog of the same colour. Her pups are always spoken for well in advance.'

'I see. In that case your concern for Fay really stemmed from the value of the pups rather than because you're genuinely fond of her.' Her voice held a hint of scorn.

'You may think as you wish, Miss—Forsyth,' he snapped icily. A silence indicated his annoyance until he said, 'Is it possible you're interested in the welfare of animals?'

'Definitely possible. Actually—there was a time when I had hopes of studying to become a vet but—but events occurred to prevent it.'

His hearty laugh broke the surrounding silence and lightened the atmosphere. '*You*——? A *vet*——?' The dark brows rose as his amused glance swept over her slender form. 'Anyone looking less like a veterinary surgeon I've yet to see. Anyhow, I don't consider it to be suitable work for a woman.'

'Indeed? Why not? There are plenty of women vets.'

'No doubt—but the majority don't last for very long.'

'I can't see why they should give up the job.' Irritated, she realised he was echoing her father's words.

'The reasons are obvious. Apart from a knowledge of stock that has to be acquired over the years, physical strength is necessary for difficult deliveries of a foal or a calf. No doubt you could shove in a needle for inoculations, but there are also heavy jobs to be handled. Or did you think you'd have a man trailing along behind to push a horse back on to its feet?'

'No, I did not,' she snapped, nettled by the derision in his tone. 'Do you think I'm a complete idiot——?'

'Then tell me this—how do you think you'd get on in

a case where a large bull has broken one horn? The animal is going mad because the jagged stump has become flyblown and is covered with maggots. The farmer rings for help from the vet station. He's told it'll be sent as soon as possible—and out comes this slip of a girl, namely, yourself. Believe me, the farmer would then become madder than his own bull.' His sarcasm lashed at her.

'You don't understand,' she protested. 'If you *must* know I had visions of a job in a veterinary clinic where I could work with smaller animals such as cats and dogs.'

'Well—that sounds more reasonable,' he admitted. 'Why didn't you take up the course? You could've gone to Massey University just out of Palmerston North.'

'Yes—I know.' She sought for an excuse. 'I—I realised I hadn't the brains for so much study and—and the difficult exams.'

'You said *events* happened to prevent it.'

'Oh—well—they were domestic. It became necessary for me to remain at home to help my mother, and at the same time I decided to learn sewing.' She fell silent, having no wish to go into these details which involved the departure of Ted and Molly from her parents' home.

'Would you like to see Fay and her pups?' he asked abruptly.

Surprised, her grey eyes shone like the depths of a still lake as a smile lit her face. 'Oh yes—please—I'd love to see them.'

'We'll ride to the homestead as soon as this shower disappears. It's becoming less and will be over in a short time because old Whariti is beginning to shed his cloak.'

As they waited for the rain to cease Julie found her eyes straying towards the silhouette of a straight nose and square jaw as Adam Malvern turned his gaze upward, watching for signs of blue sky to appear about the peak. He was a man of strength, she decided. His remote attitude seemed to be coupled with a casual exterior which indicated he couldn't care less whether she was standing beside him—or didn't even exist.

Her thoughts turned towards the hazel-eyed Elaine Brady. Who was she? Did she have a special meaning for this man? And then she brushed the question of their relationship aside. Why should she herself be giving it so much as a second thought? Her own emotions were in deep mourning for Ross Mitchell—weren't they?

And even as she became aware of his potent male sexuality she told herself there was no way in which Adam Malvern could wipe all thoughts of Ross from her mind. Yet in all honesty she had to concede that perhaps he was a man who could compensate for the loss of another, especially if a girl felt drawn towards him in some slight way. Not that *she* was, of course. Oh no—not at all.

'Come along—we'll go.' The words came as an abrupt command as he turned to leg her up into the saddle. He then mounted, and she found herself following meekly as they rode towards the gate which he again leaned down to open without bothering to dismount.

They continued along the road until they came to the entrance of a tree-lined drive where the new bronze of copper beech mingled overhead. She caught a glimpse of a white timbered, two-storeyed homestead where the misty blue of wisteria curtained the length of veranda running along the wide frontage. But before she could see more of his home Adam had led her along a side drive towards the sheds at the back.

Fay and her puppies were cosily housed in a barn away from the main kennels. The four small ones suckled their mother's bloated teats, scrambling across each other as they pushed with tiny paws. Julie knelt beside them while Adam squatted nearby. Indicating one squirming canine scrap he said, 'This fellow will be a very good dog.'

'How can you tell at this early stage?'

'By his aggressive shoving even before his eyes are open.' He laid a gentle hand on Fay's smooth head. 'Meet Miss—Forsyth, Fay. She's come to see your family.' He picked up a small furry handful and passed it to Julie.

She cuddled it against her breast, crooning over it tenderly. 'The darling wee pet—I love sheep dog puppies——'

'You can work a sheep dog?'

'No—I've never tried.'

'Fay is a heading bitch which is a special breed of Border Collie. She's been bred for the specific job of casting out widely so the sheep don't know she's there until she appears in front of them. She then controls their speed and steers them to a given place. Quite often she stays out on the wing to guide them to a gate, and at times she has the job of holding them in one place.'

She already knew the work of a heading dog, but she listened patiently, enjoying the sound of his deep voice.

'There's an old saying,' Adam went on. 'When employing a shepherd it's always wise to examine his dogs first. And incidentally, the definition of a good heading dog is one with the wiles of a woman and the will of a man.'

'The wiles of a woman?' she demanded coldly. 'You consider all women to be wily creatures?'

'I've yet to meet one who isn't. Every woman has a scheme of some sort tucked away in the back of her brain. Deception could be the second name of—of some I've met.'

The cold steel in his voice sent a chill through her. No doubt he was referring to herself. 'Is that a fact?' she flashed with a touch of anger. 'What makes you imagine that deception is the prerogative of women?'

'My observations show me that men are far more open.'

'Huh! Are you saying that men never deceive? For heaven's sake—how chauvinistic can you be?' Her voice became filled with sarcasm as she thought of Ross Mitchell, then she looked at him wonderingly. 'Why are you so bitter?'

'I'm not bitter,' he retorted coldly. 'I'm just unimpressed when I'm told lies. As Elaine said—if I discover a person has lied to me I never believe that person again.'

She bit her lip and said nothing as she stared down at the puppy nestling against her. His words had had the effect of a direct hit, making her feel uncomfortable and filling her with a sudden desire to mount Cloud and return to Molly and Ted.

Gently, she returned the pup to its mother. 'It's time I took Cloud home. Ted might begin to worry.' She stood up and crossed the yard to where the horses had been left tethered.

'You're right. He's probably wondering where you are.' He legged her up.

Mounted on Cloud she watched him throw a leg across his own saddle. 'There's no need for you to accompany me,' she informed him loftily. 'I can ride home alone.'

'Of course you can. It's just that I prefer to see that you arrive there safely.'

Julie sent him a shrewd glance. 'You mean you prefer to make sure Cloud arrives home safely,' she was goaded to reply as they rode along the drive.

'That's right,' he admitted grimly. 'How did you guess?'

'It wasn't difficult. Obviously you think more of your animals than you do of human relationships.'

'Correction. *Some* human relationships. And why not? Animals are more honest,' he said as they turned on to the road.

'Yes, you're right,' she agreed with deliberate sweetness. 'Animals never let you down. That's why I prefer horses to the majority of the men I know.'

He sent her a sharp glance. 'Those are hard words for a girl of your age. You've been let down?'

She stared straight ahead. 'You could say that—but it's something I've no intention of discussing.' Then, to change the subject, she pointed to a stand of trees with tall straight trunks and bushy needle foliage that towered to small ragged crowns. 'Aren't they white pines? I can never remember their Maori name.'

'Kahikatea. They're the tallest of our native trees but there aren't many of them left. At one time this whole area was covered with thick native bush that stretched seventy miles to the north and forty miles to the south. The trees were large because they'd been growing for hundreds of years. Their branches met overhead, allowing hardly any daylight to pierce the gloom, and in the near darkness the Maori tracks through them were narrow and difficult to negotiate.'

'It sounds eerie. I'd be terrified.' She drew a deep breath, thankful to have steered him away from the subject of her own emotional problem.

'There were many places where travellers found it necessary to slither down steep inclines, cross streams and flounder through boggy patches before scrambling up slippery banks on the other side.'

'Were your people here during those early days?'

'Yes. My great-grandfather came here during the mid-1870s when the place was being established as a junction for people travelling in various directions. To the north, south, and through the Gorge there were Scandinavian settlements, therefore it was proposed to populate The Junction, as it was then known, with English people. However, its situation in the densely wooded country soon gave it the name of Woodville.'

A deep sigh escaped her. 'It must've been a vastly different world from today.'

'Completely different. The town's first industry was timber, and then, with the felling of the bush, the pastures were laid for farming. But today there are numerous racing stables in Woodville and the town's main industry is the training of thoroughbreds. Riders take their horses to the racecourse for training every morning. And that reminds me—I'll have to see about replacing Tim. The horses must be exercised.'

She was shocked. 'You mean you'll give him the *sack*?'

'I didn't say I'd sack him.'

'You said you'd replace him.' Her grey eyes were accusing.

He became irritated. 'Dammit—I have to find someone to ride the colt. He has to be taken to the racecourse to do his work on the plough.' He gave a sigh of impatience. 'I presume you know what I mean by the plough?'

She remained silent, conscious of growing resentment. Did he imagine her to be completely ignorant? Of course she understood about the plough, but she made no interruption as he went on to explain its function.

'It's a second track inside the main track. The horses train on it. It's been ploughed, disced and harrowed so that its soft surface will make them work harder when doing pacework, and prevent their pasterns from being damaged by a hard track.'

'Perhaps I can help. I could do some pacework.'

He laughed. 'If you think I'd allow you to ride Gallant you can think again. Pacework has to be done under experienced hands.'

She made no reply. If she could ride Big Boy she could probably handle Gallant, she thought. 'Is he difficult?' she asked at last.

'Not at all—apart from the odd time when he becomes a little—er—coltish at the scent of a mare.'

She sent him an inquiring glance. 'Coltish? Oh—

yes—I see what you mean.' Her colour deepened slightly as she guessed his meaning. He himself was coltish, she thought as she sensed the virility oozing from every pore of his lean masculine form. Ross Mitchell had also been masculine, but in a different way because he lacked the magnetism of this man whose strong hands rested firmly on the reins and whose easy seat seemed to indicate he'd been born in the saddle.

'You've lived with horses all your life, Mr Malvern?' she felt compelled to ask.

'I suppose you could say so. I was given a pony at an early age, and then I became determined to ride to school. There was a school bus, but I preferred to ride. As for the stables—they were my father's hobby. He bought them from a trainer who retired to live in Palmerston North. After Dad's death I retained them, so I suppose you can say they're now my hobby.'

'Your mother—is she still living?'

'No—she died when I was fifteen years old. From then onwards Dad and I were cared for by Lucy and a series of housekeepers. Lucy was a distant relative to my mother—a forty-second cousin, Dad always declared. She's still with me, but of course she's not as young as she used to be.'

'Are any of us as young as we were?' Julie asked with a smile.

'Probably not—but most people gain a little confidence with age whereas Lucy appears to have become timid and unsure of herself.'

'Are you saying she hasn't always been timid and unsure?'

'That's right. It's a state which seems to have developed over the last couple of years. It's a sort of nervousness that wasn't there during earlier years.'

'You've no idea what has caused it?'

'I wish I did know. Perhaps it's always been there, lying under the surface. Perhaps, as a callow youth, I didn't notice it.'

'I doubt that you were ever a callow youth, Mr Malvern.'

They rode in silence until they turned into the yard of the stables where they were approached by a slim lad who walked with a definite stiffness. Julie guessed that this was Tim, the apprentice jockey, and as she dismounted she discovered him to be no taller than herself.

He grinned sheepishly at Adam. 'Good afternoon, Mr Malvern,' he said politely. 'I've got Cloud's stall all fixed for her. It's been cleaned and the straw's been spread for the night. Her oats, chaff and ground nuts are in the manger——'

'Good. Give her a rub down before you rug her up for the night.' Adam dismounted and moved to where a bay head with a white blaze down its nose appeared over the lower door of another stall. 'Hi there, Gallant—how's my boy? Is he eating well?' he demanded of Tim.

'Yes, sir—he sure is——'

No further word or look in her own direction, Julie noticed. The bay colt claimed his entire attention—not that it mattered, of course. She then became aware that Tim was looking at her reproachfully as he took Cloud's rein.

'I was getting worried about you, Miss,' he said. 'You must've gone a heck of a lot further that that ruddy white gate.'

'I was with Mr Malvern,' she explained. 'Is Ted inside?'

'Yeah—him and Mrs Lewis are having a cup of tea.' He turned to Adam with an aggrieved expression on his face. 'I've got a ruddy great boil, sir. It's right on mé ruddy——'

Julie didn't wait to learn of the boil's exact location. She hastened along the path which led from the stables to the house, entering the kitchen as Molly was about to make a fresh pot of tea.

Ted grinned at her. 'I see you've brought the boss home with you. Did you meet him on the road?'

'Yes.' She threw a quick glance towards the path then said in little more than a whisper, 'When we first met I told him my name's Julie Sterling. I didn't admit I'm a Forsyth.'

Ted's sandy brows drew together. 'Why on earth did you do that?'

'It—it was on the spur of the moment, mainly because I didn't like his manner and—and because I feared it might become worse if I admitted to being a Forsyth.'

Molly held the teapot in mid-air as she stared doubtfully at Julie. 'He won't like it when he finds out,' she warned. 'He loathes deception. He's got a real thing about it.'

'Oh—I've admitted to the Forsyth part now,' Julie assured them. 'He wasn't amused about it, and no doubt he looks on me with disgust, but it doesn't matter. I'll be out of his sight and away from here before very long.'

Ted's rugged face showed his disappointment. 'That's a pity. I was hoping you'd stay and do some riding for me. If you don't, I'm in real trouble. Young Tim now says he's got another boil coming up on the inside of his leg, and that's a real bad place. I've been phoning the various boys to see if I can replace him on a temporary basis, but at the moment they're all fully engaged. I was looking on you as a godsend,' he added dolefully.

'Of course I'll stay for as long as you wish,' Julie assured him. 'After all, Mr Malvern and I are unlikely to come in contact.'

'Good girl,' Ted approved. 'By the way, why were you so long in walking Cloud to the gate and back?'

'Mr Malvern and I sheltered from the rain and then he took me to see Fay and her pups.'

A rapid glance shot between Molly and Ted. 'He

actually took you to see Fay? Well, I'll be damned,' Ted exclaimed.

Further discussion was curtailed by the sound of Adam Malvern's step on the back veranda, and as he entered the kitchen Molly handed him a cup of tea.

'Thank you, Molly, that's just what I need.' He turned to Ted and their talk centred around the horses and the problem of Tim's present inability to ride. 'You'll have to find someone to do Gallant's pacework in the morning,' he said. 'There's sure to be an apprentice jockey sitting in Woodville with nothing to do.'

'Yes—sure to be,' Ted muttered staring into his cup.

'Well—see who you can find.'

'Sure—I'll do that,' Ted agreed.

Watching them as she sipped her tea Julie again noticed that Adam Malvern neither looked in her direction nor appeared to give her a second thought. It was as though she didn't exist. However, while he ignored her she was able to study him, and once more she found herself comparing him with Ross Mitchell.

Never in his life had Ross looked as handsome as this tall dark man with the regular features that stemmed from good bone structure. But nor was Ross so offhand and abrupt to a point almost amounting to rudeness. Yet with Adam she at least knew where she stood. It was obvious she hadn't even remotely impressed him, and she was therefore unlikely to find a place in his interest, whereas with Ross—right from the first moment of meeting—she had been led along to imagine she meant a great deal to him.

Depressed, she wandered out to the back veranda where she stood watching a black tui sipping honey from the yellow bell-like flowers of a kowhai tree.

Molly came to stand beside her. 'Adam's a man of definite decisions,' she whispered. 'He walks a straight line without stepping aside, and once his mind's made up it usually remains unchanged.'

'I can believe it,' Julie agreed, recalling that Ross, on the other hand, was inclined to dither between different courses that could be taken.

Molly gazed up at the bird. 'That tui thinks he owns that tree. He chases all other birds out of it. See the tuft of white feathers at his throat? He's also called the parson bird.'

But Julie was no longer interested in the bird as she realised that dithering had been Ross's trouble concerning Anna and herself. He loved them both but he'd been undecided and plagued with uncertainty when choosing between them until finally he'd chosen Anna. But was he now definitely sure that Anna was the right one for him? It was a disturbing thought because Ross had so often been known to change his mind.

She turned and leaned her back against the veranda rail, the change of position giving her a clear view of the two men sitting at the table. Their heads were bent over the thoroughbred stud-book, and she knew they were comparing it with the catalogue from the last yearling sale.

A shaft of sunlight fell across Adam's hair, making it gleam like the black wing of the tui, and she had an almost irresistible desire to lay her hand on it, to feel its texture. But even as she controlled the impulse he looked up and met her gaze.

It was a long unseeing stare that gave her the impression he was looking right through her; then, as he turned again to Ted and the low murmur of his voice came to her ears she knew it had taken only one meeting with this man to erase all longing for Ross.

Suddenly, and without a shadow of doubt, it had disappeared right out of her heart. What was the matter with her? Was she also a bundle of changeable uncertainty?

CHAPTER THREE

JULIE was slightly shocked by her own infidelity when she realised she was no longer in a state of mental stress over Ross Mitchell. It hadn't taken long to get over him, she told herself wryly, and while she was almost willing to admit that Adam Malvern had shown her a more fascinating type of man—a man who could make a girl's heart thump—she would not concede that he had anything to do with her emotional recovery.

No—it was as Mother had said—she had been in need of fresh fields, and it was the change of environment that had given her something new to think about. That evening she was even able to speak in a casual manner about Anna's engagement, and when she went to bed she felt relaxed and happy as she set the alarm for an early hour because she was going to the track with Ted.

It was barely daylight when the alarm rang in her ear, but she sprang out of bed and dressed hurriedly in a warm brown polo-neck jersey and her jodhpurs. But as she almost ran through the kitchen Molly barred her way.

'Just you draw rein, young Julie—you'll have something to eat before you go out with those horses.'

'But Ted will be waiting——'

'Let him wait. That's an order.' Molly's tone was sharp. 'I'm not sure he's doing the right thing by allowing you to do this pacework. I reckon the boss'll be mad if he finds out. He's got odd ideas—especially about girls taking up jockey work.'

'I've no intention of taking up jockey work,' Julie pointed out as she ate the toast that was liberally spread with Molly's home-made marmalade. 'I'm only helping Ted out of a hole.'

When she reached the stables both horses stood waiting, the rattling of their bits and impatient little stamps indictating they were alert and ready to go. Ted legged her up into Gallant's exercise saddle, then handed her Cloud's bridle rein.

'The racecourse isn't far away,' he said. 'I'll drive ahead slowly in the small truck and you can follow at a walking pace. 'You'll find Gallant to be a nice easy fellow.'

Tim, who had already begun cleaning out the stalls, threw two day-rugs on to the back of the truck. He looked up at her with pleading eyes. 'If any of them ruddy boys asks why I aren't on Gallant—don't tell them anything. They'll think it's a hell of a joke—me with ruddy boils. Will you promise?'

'I promise,' she assured him as she left the yard.

Turning on to the road the chill of the early October morning struck sharply against her cheeks as she walked Gallant and led Cloud. The horses seemed to know where they were going because they stepped along briskly as they followed the familiar vehicle in front of them.

At the racecourse Ted left the truck on the roadside. He then guided her through the horse entrance gates to a row of open stalls, some of them already occupied by horses that watched their approach by looking over the chain drawn across the fronts. Cloud was put in one of the empty stalls.

Ted then led Julie and Gallant away from the stalls towards the course, and as they crossed the main track to the plough he gave her instructions. 'Take him round twice at half pace. Have you done it recently for your father?'

'No—not for ages. We have very little to do with his trainer these days. It's not like the old days when you were there, but don't worry, I think I can still judge half pace.'

She could see other horses working on the plough, some of the boys riding in pairs, others in threes, their voices floating on the still air as they laughed and shouted ribald remarks to each other.

She reined Gallant as she waited for two groups to pass, then, giving into his small impatient rears, she allowed him to be on his way. He was responsive and an easy horse to work although she found him difficult to hold; therefore, to keep him at half pace she bridged the reins by holding them firmly down on his neck. Gallant was then pulling against himself. He got the message and after a few strides he settled down to steady pacework.

The two rounds flitted past rapidly and she enjoyed the exhilaration of the ride. She was also aware of inquisitive stares coming from some of the boys but she took no notice of them, and when she reached the plough gate for the second time she found Ted waiting for her.

'Good girl,' he remarked with satisfaction. 'I can see you haven't lost the art.' His hand on the rein, he led the colt back to the stall where Cloud stood waiting. The exercise saddle was transferred from Gallant to the grey filly, and as Julie rode her towards the plough Ted began the process of hosing down Gallant.

Cloud was delighted to be given a run. She did her share of pulling and the same rein-bridging tactics had to be applied to keep her speed down. However, it was a strain, and by the time Julie was on her second round the effort of holding first one and then the other horse at half pace was taking its toll on her limited strength. Her arms were aching from the constant pressure on the reins, and her knees were becoming sore.

Her presence had now been noticed by most of the other riders, and this fact became clear as three of them drew abreast of her near the members' stand. They stared at her intently.

Said one, 'There you are—I *told* you it's a girl. Can't you see she's got *boobs*——?'

Julie flushed scarlet but ignored them.

'What you doin' tonight, Lady Godiva?' laughed the second boy.

'You goin' to be one of them smart-aleck female jockeys?' demanded the third. 'We'll ride the lot of you off the track——'

'Hey—where's Tim?' shouted the first boy. 'Why aren't he ridin' Cloud? Are you tryin' to do him out of a job?'

She continued to ignore them, thankful that the plough gate was near, but at the same time she became perturbed by the sight of a lone figure standing near it. Even from the distance she could see the tall form did not belong to Ted. It was Adam Malvern.

His brow was dark, his mouth set in a hard thin line. 'Where the devil's Ted?' he snapped coldly.

Taking no notice of his attitude she asked sweetly, 'Isn't he at the stalls? I left him hosing down Gallant.'

His brow became even darker. '*Gallant?* Are you telling me you've already had Gallant round the plough?'

Defiance came to her aid. 'Why not? It isn't the first time I've exercised a thoroughbred on the plough.'

His eyes narrowed as they surveyed her. 'Yet, when walking Cloud yesterday, you allowed me to explain about the plough. You let me think you knew nothing about it. Why such deliberate deception?'

'Correction. There was no deception. You *assumed* I know nothing about it. For Pete's sake—you went on and on about it. I thought it'd be rude to interrupt.'

'Did you, indeed?' he retorted grimly. 'Are you sure you weren't having a damned good giggle at my expense?'

'Believe it or not, Mr Malvern, I did not find you even remotely amusing. On the contrary, I found you to be rather boringly full of yourself.'

'Thank you.' The words were almost a snarl.

They made their way back to the stalls in silence until
at last she felt compelled to say, 'Please don't be angry
with Ted. He did his best to find a rider for this
morning. He rang first one boy and then another, but
there didn't seem to be anyone available.'

He made no reply.

As they reached the stalls Ted glanced at his set face.
'Good morning, Boss,' he said cheerfully. 'We're sure
lucky to have this lass on tap, otherwise there'd have
been no plough work done this morning and these
horses must be kept in trim. Did you watch her go
round?'

'Yes—I watched her.' Adam's tone was abrupt.

'Then you'll have noticed how happy the horses are
with her,' Ted was quick to point out. 'She's got good
hands—but you'll have noticed that for yourself.'

'I watched her with Cloud but I don't like the idea of
her up on Gallant. Nor do I wish to hear of it again,
especially when he's due to be given fast work.'

'She can ride him, Boss,' Ted declared with stubborn
confidence as he turned the hose on Cloud's legs.

But his words of assurance brought no answer from
Adam Malvern who turned abruptly and left the stalls.
Nor did he favour Julie with as much as a glance.

Ted grinned at her. 'Don't let him worry you. He's
got a temper but it never lasts for long.'

Her chin rose. 'Why should it worry me?'

'Why, indeed?' he chuckled. 'Why should his presence
bring the colour to your cheeks and make your eyes
sparkle? Or did you imagine I hadn't noticed?'

The horses were walked home with Julie riding Cloud
and leading Gallant. She felt disgruntled and decided
the Malvern man was being thoroughly unreasonable.
She also told herself she didn't like him, and as for
Ted's stupid suggestion that his presence had an effect
upon her—it was just a lot of rot and also completely
ridiculous.

They reached the stables without incident and as she dismounted Ted noticed her stiffness. 'A hot bath is what you need,' he advised. 'Go and lie in one and then Molly will give you some breakfast. Off you go before Adam returns——'

He was teasing her of course, but she hurried towards the bathroom lest his words proved to be correct and Adam *did* return. Minutes later she was lying stretched in the hot water which acted like a miracle. The stiffness disappeared from her arms and legs, and by the time she'd towelled her hair and sprayed herself lavishly with Chanel eau de Cologne she felt better.

She had not brought many clothes with her, but the fine woollen misty-blue gathered skirt and matching lacy knitted top with its frilled neck and cuffs gave her a softly feminine appearance, while the final touch of make-up endowed her with much needed confidence.

As she entered the kitchen she sensed that Molly was about to begin a quiet and tactful probing for the reason for her sudden desire to visit them. After all, she'd been here for hours without a word of explanation, but, strangely, she no longer felt the need to cry on Molly's ample shoulder. Therefore, by way of forestalling awkward questions, she began with a query that had been niggling at the back of her own mind.

'Who is Elaine Brady?' she asked. She had wanted to bring the question forward the previous evening but had hesitated to sound too curious about Adam Malvern's friends.

'Elaine?' Molly turned the pikelets beginning to bubble on the circular iron plate. 'She's really the housekeeper. She's supposed to be Lucy's companion help, but because of their age difference there's very little companionship.'

'Then why not employ someone nearer Lucy's age?'

'I think Adam gave her the job because their parents had been old friends, and at least she's proved herself to be an excellent housekeeper. Everything is kept in spick and span order, to say nothing of the attention she dances on *him*!'

'They must be—very old friends.'

'Yes. Did you meet Lucy?'

'No.' Then to Molly's unspoken question, 'I met Elaine when we sheltered from the rain. She was out riding.'

'Oh.' Molly spooned more mixture on to the iron plate. 'She's got a good job, has that one. A horse provided and a Mini at her disposal. It's no wonder people expect them to be married sooner or later.'

Julie was conscious of an inward jar. 'Do *you* expect them to marry? I mean—is there something between them——?'

Molly shrugged. 'I'll believe it when I see the ceremony take place—and not before.'

Half an hour later a green Peugeot swung into the yard. Adam stepped from it, his arrival causing the colour to flood into Julie's cheeks. Earlier, when leaving the racecourse, he had been in such an angry mood she had not expected to see him again quite so soon. Nor did he look particularly pleased now, and she wondered if he'd come to further reprimand Ted for having put her up on Gallant. But more surprise was in store when she realised it wasn't Ted he'd come to see. It was herself.

His manner was quiet as he strode into the kitchen, and in a voice that brooked no argument he said, 'I've come to take you home to lunch.'

'To lunch? *Me?*' She gaped at him, unable to find further words to cope with his high-handedness, but conscious of the quickening of her heartbeat. Nor did she intend to let him see she was delighted by the invitation, and this made it difficult to keep the smile of pleasure from her face. Forcing herself to look at him gravely she said, 'This is an unexpected surprise, Mr Malvern.'

'Well—it's Lucy,' he explained gravely. 'She was

quite put out yesterday. Apparently she saw us from an upstairs window when I took you to see Fay and her pups. She fully expected me to bring you in to meet her, and when we didn't appear she was disappointed.'

'Why should she wish to meet me?' Julie asked, her grey eyes reflecting the blue of her jersey as she looked inquiringly at Adam.

'Because she meets so few people,' he explained. 'Therefore anyone she does happen to meet is a highlight in her day.'

Molly sent him a teasing smile. 'She also likes to meet any new female who happens to loom on Adam's horizon.'

'Then she needn't fear for him as far as I'm concerned.' Julie's sharp tone held more force than she intended.

Adam looked at her with unconcealed amusement. 'I should warn you that Molly's right. Lucy considers it to be more than high time I got married. She's longing to see at least half a dozen children's ponies out in the paddock or tethered in the yard, and she's afraid she'll die before she sees even one.'

'Is she ill?' Julie asked.

'Not really—although there are times when I wonder if she isn't keeping quiet about a secret ailment of some sort.'

'Or if an ailment of some sort hasn't been planted in her mind,' Molly suggested shrewdly.

He was silent for several long moments. 'Now where would you get an idea like that?' he demanded at last.

'Where indeed?' she prevaricated. 'These ideas are inclined to spring out of the top of my head for no reason at all.'

His jaw tightened slightly. 'Are you hinting that Elaine would plant such an idea in her head?'

Molly's plump shoulders lifted in a shrug. 'I'm hinting at nothing. I'm merely saying that if Lucy thinks she has an ailment it's either real or false—and if it's false the idea has had to come from somewhere. Right?'

The fact that Molly's words had given him something to think about was proved by his silence as the Peugeot sped along the road. Nor could Julie find the courage to interrupt his thoughts, therefore she kept her eyes straight ahead although she had only to turn her head slightly to see the firm, well-shaped hands resting on the wheel, and the outline of the handsome features chiselled by his good bone structure.

She was also aware of the excited flow of her own bloodstream. She knew that her cheeks were flushed and she made no attempt to deny that the reason was all wrapped up with this man. Turning a little she could see the firm curve of his lips, and it took only an atom of instinct to tell her that his kiss would be very different from the half friendly, half passionate caress pressed on her mouth by Ross Mitchell.

They had almost reached the homestead drive before his silence was broken by a remark which caused her to catch her breath. His voice cool, he said, 'During lunch I intend to call you Julie—and you'll call me Adam.'

It was an order which had no by-your-leave about it, she noticed as he went on with further explanation.

'Lucy is Mrs Taylor, but she prefers to be called Lucy because she imagines it makes her feel younger. It also gives us an easier atmosphere, but of course if you really object I'll understand——'

'Not at all. Nor am I keen on being called Miss Forsyth,' she admitted as the car stopped beside the front steps where mauve wistaria curtained the veranda.

Lucy had been watching for their arrival. She came through the front door to greet them, a small frail woman with grey hair and soft brown eyes that were alive with interest as they regarded Julie. Smiling, she held out her hand.

'I saw you yesterday from the window. I watched you nurse a puppy and I said to myself—now there's a girl who loves animals. I was so disappointed when Adam didn't bring you in to meet me.'

'Would you believe she wanted to become a vet?' Adam said in mocking tones.

A voice spoke from behind them. 'What a ghastly job for a girl.'

They turned as Elaine came up the veranda steps. Her hair no longer hung loosely but was secured in a style that gave her a sophisticated air, and Julie now saw that she was tall. In one hand she carried stems of pink flowering cherry, while the other was extended in greeting as though to establish the fact that she was the true hostess in this house. 'Shall we go inside?' she suggested, ushering Julie in with the easy grace of the lady of the manor.

Julie glanced at Lucy as they followed Elaine into the lounge. Did the small woman look slightly irritated—or was this her own imagination? And then her interest was caught by the interior of the room they had entered. The spacious area was covered with paisley patterned wall-to-wall carpet and furnished with settees and armchairs of large and comfortable design. Several oil paintings hung from the walls, each one being the portrait of a Maori of earlier days when most of them wore flax or kiwi feathered cloaks and had the dark blue spirals of tattoo on their faces.

Lucy followed Julie's gaze as she moved about the room examining first one and then another of the portraits. 'They're all the work of Lindauer,' she explained.

'Lindauer?' Julie's eyes went to Elaine who'd said she'd waited at the Lindauer. 'Isn't that the name of a restaurant?'

'It is,' Adam said. 'People often arrange to meet there.'

She turned to look at him, then flushed as she realised he was regarding her with amusement.

'It was named after Gottfried Lindauer,' Lucy

explained. 'He was an artist who came from Bohemia. He settled in Woodville where he became quite famous for his accurate paintings of the Maori people. This woman with the baby on her back is Ana Rupene who lived in the Thames district. He painted several of her.'

'He was friendly with my grandfather,' Adam explained. He moved to stand beside her as she looked up at Ana Rupene. 'What is she thinking about with that half-smile on her face? Let your feminine instinct run riot and tell me what she'd say if she could speak. Take note of the twinkle in her eyes.'

Julie examined the brown face with its short straight black hair. The skin colouring was like coffee with a dash of cream, while clever brush strokes had placed touches of light and shade to give a pleased expression to the eyes and mouth. The baby had chubby cheeks and a look of contentment as he peeped over the deep cream cloak of woven flax which held him safely to his mother's back.

'I think she's a happy woman,' she said at last. 'She's saying, this is my little one—he's all I need.'

He moved to stand closer as he murmured in her ear, 'You're wrong. She's not saying that at all. She's looking at a man who has just told her he'll see her later. Her smile is his answer.'

She was startled by the intensity of his tone. It was almost as though the message had been directed towards herself—and then commonsense rapidly asserted itself, causing her to shake her head. 'I don't believe that for one moment. She's just completely happy with her baby.'

'Nonsense. The title of the painting should be *See You Later*.'

She glanced about nervously, fearing that Lucy had heard his words which seemed to have a strange meaning behind them, but that small person had moved through a wide archway which divided the lounge from the dining-room.

'Yes—definitely—*see you later*,' he said again, his voice still low as he emphasised the words.

Her grey eyes widened with surprise as they turned to meet the shadowed depths of his own, and then something hypnotic about their darkness held her gaze until she felt almost powerless to drag it away. Nor could she understand the slight tremor that gripped her.

The spell was broken by Lucy's plaintive voice floating through the archway. Complaining to Elaine she said, 'I think cherry blossom is too large for a table centre. I'll not be able to see beyond it. Couldn't we have something small in a low bowl?'

'You'll just have to peep round it,' Elaine told her calmly and without making a move to alter the table floral arrangement.

'Well—really——'

Julie's ears caught the sigh of exasperation that escaped Lucy, and it was this small incident which betrayed the older woman's secret ailment referred to by Adam. It was, she suspected, a case of frustration and unhappiness.

Watching her closely Julie realised that Lucy's cherished position had been usurped. She was no longer mistress in this house where she'd reigned for years, nor, it seemed, had she the aggressiveness and strength necessary to regain her former authority. A feeling of sympathy for Lucy filled her, causing her to cross the room and sit beside her on the settee. 'We'll peep at each other through the flowers,' she smiled.

Adam poured sherries. 'She's longing to know all about you,' he said with a wry grin as he handed her a stemmed crystal glass. 'Especially your potential as a——'

'Stop it, Adam,' Lucy snapped indignantly. 'You're making me sound like an inquisitive old woman,' she protested.

He gave a short laugh. 'Now be honest, Lucy. You're

just busting to ask Julie about her home and to learn about her parents.'

But Lucy's moment of learning about Julie's parents was turned aside by Elaine whose hazel eyes glowed earnestly as they rested upon Adam. 'I don't believe Lucy's even remotely interested in Julie's affairs,' she told him. 'It's the outside world she wants to know about.'

He frowned. 'Outside world? What on earth are you talking about? She's not a prisoner.'

Elaine gave a small shrug. 'She might as well be, considering her lack of social contact. Apart from you—at rare moments—and me, when I'm not busy, she hardly sees a soul, not even the people who work on the farm.' She turned to the older woman. 'Isn't that so, Lucy? Isn't your life a lonely one?'

'Well—yes—there are times when I'm rather lonely,' Lucy confessed with reluctance. 'But I don't mind,' she added hastily.

'There you are—what she needs is *company*.' Elaine's eyes held a gleam of triumph.

'Can't you give her a small amount?' Adam drawled lazily.

'I think Lucy would be the first to admit we're not exactly on the same wavelength,' she returned coolly.

His brows drew together. 'What's that supposed to mean?'

Elaine took a final sip from her sherry glass before she uncrossed her long shapely legs and stood up. 'I suppose it's really the generation gap,' she sighed, sending him a faint smile. 'Excuse me—I'll serve lunch.'

Silence fell as she left the room, walking with the elegance and grace of a highly trained model. Julie looked at Lucy who had suddenly become rather tight-lipped, and then her glance slid towards Adam who sat with his legs stretched before him, still frowning as he studied the toes of his expensive English shoes.

Was there actual antagonism between Lucy and Elaine? she wondered. Surely, Adam would refuse to tolerate such a situation unless—unless he had a special feeling for Elaine. And if this was a fact it would contribute to Lucy's secret ailment.

The thoughts filled her with depression. Elaine, living in the house with him, had every opportunity to become more than a mere housekeeper for Adam. In the dark of the night he had only to walk along a passage or across a hall to one of those upstairs rooms—and no doubt he'd find her waiting for him, her hair loosened to allow the dark locks to fall about her shoulders, her scanty nightdress revealing a body that called to his male needs.

So what? she asked herself angrily as the picture built itself in her mind. Why should she care? Yet she knew she *did* care.

When they sat at the table Elaine again took over the role of hostess by cutting into the tasty asparagus quiche and serving the tossed salad and rolls of ham. She also kept up a flow of chatter, deftly drawing Julie into the conversation.

'Are you wondering how I recognised you as being a Forsyth?' she asked sweetly.

'Not really.' Julie managed to look unconcerned. She had no wish to have this particular subject dragged up again.

'I'll tell you just the same,' Elaine went on. 'I saw you at the races the day Big Boy beat our Gallant. You were with Big Boy's owner Mr Forsyth, whom I knew by sight, and I noticed the smart green suit you were wearing. Did you buy it in Palmerston North?'

'No. I made it myself.' Then, in an effort to change the subject, 'I bought the material in Palmy because I go there quite often. I have aunts living there. One of them—Great-aunt Helen—lives in a pensioner flat.'

'She does?' Elaine was suddenly interested and her questions came eagerly. 'Is she happy in it? Is it near the town? Can she walk to the shops or to an afternoon film?'

Julie looked at her thoughtfully, surprised by her curiosity. 'Yes—my great-aunt is very happy in her flat. She walks to the shops and has the company of others living in the block, most of whom are about her own age.'

'There now——' Elaine sent a triumphant glance towards Lucy, smiling a little but not pressing the point.

'I—I think I'd be nervous—living alone in a flat,' Lucy said with a slight tremor in her voice.

Elaine gave her a reassuring smile. 'That's nonsense. You wouldn't be nervous with other people living close to you.' She turned to Julie, her finely arched brows raised. 'I'm sure your great-aunt isn't at all nervous?'

'Not at all—but that's because she has one of my cousins living with her. My aunts don't believe in elderly people living alone, so they make sure there's always someone with her.'

'Oh—I see——' Elaine sounded deflated.

Lucy's voice came tremulously. 'Your great-aunt is very fortunate to be taken care of.'

Adam leaned forward to place a hand on her thin arm. 'Don't let anything worry you, Lucy,' he comforted her. 'You'll never be left to fend for yourself.'

Elaine became very still. Her fork with its morsel of food was held momentarily in midair, then replaced untouched on the plate before her while her eyes seemed to study the tablecloth.

Watching her discreetly the situation was suddenly clear to Julie, and she knew that by mentioning the pensioner flats she'd inadvertently played right into Elaine's hands. Elaine, she guessed, was no longer satisfied with having taken over Lucy's position, and it seemed that she now wanted her right out of the house.

Lucy, Julie feared, was well aware of this fact, and, obviously, it was all part of her secret ailment, giving an added inner apprehension that gnawed at her sense of security and kept her in a state of nervous tension.

She sent Adam a veiled glance. Was he also aware of Elaine's plans? If so, what was his attitude towards them? The enigmatic quality of his expression told her nothing.

The long silence which had fallen after his last words made Julie feel it was time to steer the conversation away from the household's private problems. Horses would be a normal topic, she decided, therefore she turned to Adam and said, 'Ted will be expecting me to walk Cloud and Gallant this afternoon.'

He brushed the suggestion aside. 'There's no need for you to be concerned about them. I've arranged for Ted to do the job himself, so they'll be in good hands.'

Julie felt a spark of indignation. 'Are you saying you're not happy when they're in my hands?'

'No—I didn't mean that. In fact your riding capabilities have more than surprised me. They're very good.'

His remark pleased Lucy. 'There now—he's *praised* you. He seldom gives praise to anyone.'

'The cook least of all,' Elaine commented dryly.

'That's not true,' Lucy assured her kindly. 'I happen to know he appreciates you more than you realise.'

'Really? You could've fooled me,' Elaine smiled, her eyes betraying a glow of pleasure before her lids were lowered.

During the remainder of the meal Julie concentrated upon talking to Lucy. After all it was what she was here for, and she had the satisfaction of watching the small woman brighten visibly as she spoke of her own earlier days at Malvern. Then, just as lunch was almost over, the phone rang.

Adam excused himself and left the table to answer it. When he returned he said, 'That was Jack Cameron. He thinks we should buy some of those ewes being sold from the Jordan estate, and he also suggests that Dixie

and Dell should be given a spell up on Whariti.' He
turned to Julie, adding by way of explanation, 'Jack
Cameron's my farm manager.'

Julie looked at him with a question in her grey eyes.
'Who—or what—are Dixie and Dell?'

Elaine laughed. 'Hasn't he told you about his precious
brood mares? They're the most important females in his
life. Even Lucy will agree with me on that point.'

Adam merely grinned at Elaine, nor did he deny the
accusation. Instead he said, 'It means I must take a
drive to the back of the property to examine the
pastures. I know old Whariti's been generous with his
spring rains, but we can't pile extra ewes on the place
unless we have sufficient feed for them.'

Elaine said, 'The last time I rode out there the feed
appeared to be knee-deep——'

Ignoring the suggestion that the drive to the back
area was really unnecessary, Adam turned to Julie.
'Would you care to come with me?'

She tried to keep the eagerness from her voice. 'Oh
yes—I'd love to.'

He then turned to Lucy, his manner polite. 'Would
you like to come with us, Lucy? It's ages since you've
had a run out on the farm. You've probably forgotten
what the back hills are like.'

Lucy was silent for a moment, then, looking from
Adam to Julie she said, 'No thank you. I feel a little
tired. I'm sure I'd be wiser to have my afternoon
rest.'

He turned again to Julie. 'You're sure you won't be
bored by such mundane activity?'

But before she could answer Elaine cut in with a
short laugh as she stood up to clear the table, her
quick deft movements betraying an underlying irritation.

'She won't be bored if you show her all the
interesting places you once showed *me*,' she told Adam
with a touch of bitterness.

She then sent Julie a smouldering glance of dislike before wheeling the trolley from the room, and if her barely concealed anger was noticed by Adam he ignored it.

CHAPTER FOUR

THE green Peugeot ran along the farm road, making light work of the bumps and hollows in the metal surface. On either side the lush pastures were being grazed by prime cattle, their smooth black hides gleaming in the sun, and by sheep which were heavily fleeced with wool. Several good riding-hacks raised their heads in curiosity as they passed.

Pointing to one of them Adam said, 'That chestnut gelding is the one Elaine usually rides.'

Why did the thought of Elaine riding beside him send prickles of resentment through her? Julie wondered.

'The season's been kind this year,' he went on with satisfaction. 'Whariti's been generous with his rain and the fresh feed is coming along nicely.'

'Yes—it is——' Her thoughts were not really with the state of the pastures; instead they had switched to Elaine's last words which were now mulling about in her mind.

She won't be bored if you show her all the interesting places you've shown me, she had said.

What and where were these interesting places? She stared about the countryside as the car made its way between the rising contour of hills, but she could see nothing that was particuarly interesting, or even vaguely out of the ordinary.

She was also acutely aware of the close proximity of Adam and the effect he was having upon her emotions. From the corner of her eye she could see his strong hands keeping a firm grip on the wheel, and she almost jumped when he moved to point out a building which nestled within the shelter of trees.

'We call that the staff house,' he explained. 'Jack

Cameron and his wife Mary live in it, and they give accommodation to Ray Jones, a young shepherd who works with Jack.'

They passed a tall open-sided Dutch barn, its store of winter hay now depleted, and a short distance further on they came to the woolshed which was protected from the strong westerly winds by an ancient plantation of pines. The large weatherboard building was painted a dark red with white facings, and surrounded by yards divided by white rails. Behind the shed stood a large round concrete tank which stored the water supply.

'It's a four-stand shed,' Adam told her. 'You can either come in and have a look at it, or you can wait here while I speak to Jack and Ray. They're having a clean up in the shed before the shearing gang arrives at the end of this month.'

'I'll wait here, thank you——'

'Okay—suit yourself.' His tone had become abrupt.

He left the car and she sat watching his back as his long strides took him towards the shed. She saw him mount the front steps to the loading platform, then disappear into the gloom beyond the wide-open door.

The bleat of a sheep floated on the air, but apart from its plaintive cry the surrounding hills held an eerie silence that seemed to be impregnated with loneliness. She became aware that his absence from the car was filling her with a vague feeling of desolation, and the next instant something stronger than herself had forced her to open the door and make her way towards the shed.

Climbing the steps and entering the building she realised it was similar to the one at home, except that her father's woolshed was a three-stand and therefore slightly smaller than this four-stand shed. However, the same type of machines were there, hanging from the overhead rod and waiting for the turn of the switch that would set them buzzing while the wool was being shorn. The wooltable, where the fleeces would be spread while being skirted for anything that should be removed, was the same, and, as at home, the woolpress stood waiting to receive the rolled bundles of wool.

A glance towards a corner of the shed showed Adam engrossed with a man she presumed to be Jack Cameron. They appeared to be discussing the number of woolpacks on hand, and, rather than force an introduction, she went outside again to the loading platform. As she did so a young man in his late teens came up the steps.

He stood still at the sight of her. 'Hullo—are you looking for someone?' he asked, running a hand through red tousled hair while a grin split his freckled face. Then, glancing towards the Peugeot, 'Oh—you've come with the boss?'

'Yes.' This must be Ray Jones, she decided.

He gave a low whistle as his admiring eyes flicked over her face and form. 'Gosh—you're a good looker— does Elaine know you're out with him?'

She looked at him dumbly, unable to think of anything to say.

'You'd better watch out if she catches you with him,' he warned.

She swept him with a cold glare. 'Aren't you being somewhat presumptous? Suppose you mind your own business——'

'Okay—okay—no offence meant. I was only saying what I think.'

She pushed past him and went down the steps, the words echoing in her mind and making her realise that even this shepherd expected Adam and Elaine to marry. Still, it wasn't surprising. Elaine had both beauty and dignity, and wasn't she already gracing the homestead as though she were its mistress?

The suggestion that anyone could supplant Elaine— least of all herself—suddenly seemed to be quite ridiculous. 'Most unlikely——' she said, voicing her thoughts aloud.

'What's most unlikely?' Adam spoke from behind her.

Startled, she swung round to face him. The colour rushed to her face and she found it necessary to turn away again.

'Well—what's most unlikely?' he persisted.

Her mind groped wildly in various directions, then her eyes fell on the large concrete water tank. Pointing to its top she said, 'It appears to be covered over, so it's not likely to be filled by rainwater. Or is there a spring nearby——?'

He looked at her doubtfully. 'Is that what you were really thinking about?'

'What would you suggest I was thinking about?' she countered.

He shook his head a trifle vaguely. 'The female mind is a deep mystery to me. I wouldn't even try to understand it. As for the tank—its water is piped from a large spring in the hills. If you're wearing suitable shoes I'll show it to you.' Looking down at her feet he nodded approval.

They continued along the farm road which rose gradually to higher ground until the track dwindled and almost disappeared. At last, with the Peugeot bumping over rough grass, Adam stopped the car. He got out and opened the passenger seat door for her.

'This is as far as we'll drive,' he said. 'I don't want to risk getting stuck in a patch of boggy ground. There are numerous small springs in this area and they're difficult to locate at this time of the year when everything is so green.'

She got out and looked about her. 'We're higher than I thought. Do we follow a track? I can't see one.'

'There used to be a well-defined track but over the years it's disappeared mainly because so few people come here now.' He pointed to an area of bush fairly high up on a steep hillside. 'We'll head for that clump of trees up there. Do you think you can climb so far?'

'Of course—so long as the ground's not too slippery,' she declared valiantly, yet feeling doubtful.

Difficulties began when they reached the higher level. The soles of her shoes were too smooth for the ground's damp surface, and after she had slithered in a bad patch Adam took a firm grip on her hand. His touch sent quivers down her spine, making her heart thump and causing a state of breathlessness that was not entirely due to the steepness of the hill.

At last they reached the trees where, to her surprise, a large dark hole loomed in the hillside. The wind sighed softly in the branches surrounding it, and from somewhere came the ripples and splashes of running water.

'It's a cave!' she exclaimed.

'More than a cave,' he corrected. 'It's a cave with a well. See how the falling water has formed a deep hole in the rocky floor. It must've been going on for thousands of years.' He stared upwards. 'Look—it comes from up there——'

She stepped back to gaze up at the small steady stream pouring from a narrow hole high in the cave's wall, and as she did so her foot slid on a slimy patch of the uneven floor. A small gasp escaped her as she made a sudden backward lunge, but a strong arm was flung round her waist and she was dragged against Adam's body.

The near-fall left her in a state of momentary shock, causing her to cling to him gratefully until she said in a small shaky voice, 'Thank you—I almost landed in the mud——'

He did not reply, and as she waited for him to release her she became aware that he stared down into her face, his features barely discernible in the gloom of the cave.

Wordlessly, she returned his gaze as though answering an unspoken demand. His arm had remained firmly round her waist, and then, startled, she realised his other arm had crept about her, enfolding her in an embrace which held her even closer to him.

The unexpectedness of it made her nerves tingle, while a rapid intake of breath betrayed her leaping pulses as she felt the solidness of his chest, the hard muscles of his thighs.

'Julie—oh, Julie——' he murmured, his voice low and husky.

She knew his hands were gliding slowly up and down her spine, gently massaging her back as he pressed her against him, and, throwing restraint aside her arms went up to entwine about his neck. It was a gesture of submission she was unable to withhold, and as she raised her face his hard mouth came down to plunder her soft parted lips in a kiss that made her world stand still.

Flames leapt through her veins, reducing to ashes any willpower she might have used to resist his embrace—nor did she have any desire to repulse the moulding of his body against her own. Vaguely she knew she should make an effort to push him away, but she was like a rag doll, hypnotised beneath the spell of his magnetism, and enraptured by the feel of his arms about her, his lips on her own.

'You're a devastating little witch—you're setting me on fire,' he muttered in her ear—then he kissed her again with an ardour that left her gasping.

Until these moments Julie had been unaware that she possessed such dormant fires within her own body. Her previous experience, which had consisted mainly of Ross Mitchell's lukewarm caresses, had left her ill-equipped to cope with the onslaught of passion that now encompassed and coursed through her entire being like a stream of red-hot lava, and for several mad minutes she allowed herself to float in a mist of bliss.

The spell was broken when his lips left her mouth to wander across her face and nuzzle the lobe of her ear. The uncontrolled whirlwind of thoughts racing through her mind began to untangle themselves into a vague semblance of mental coherence, and with it came sufficient sanity to bring her down to earth.

'Please, Adam—please stop——' She withdrew her arms from about his neck while her hands made futile attempts to free herself from his embrace. Turning her face away from the lips that again sought her own she whispered, 'This is ridiculous——'

He gave a soft laugh. 'Ridiculous isn't the word I'd place upon it,' he murmured huskily, his lips again wandering across her cheeks. 'You don't know what you do to me—you're so lovely——'

'But so stupid—and so very surprised at myself.' She turned away, fearing the dangers of another emotional upheaval. 'You had no right to—to kiss me like—like that.'

'But you knew it would happen,' he declared in a low voice.

The words startled her, causing her to turn and stare at him in angry amazement. 'I did? How on earth would I know? Do you imagine I'm clairvoyant?'

'Didn't I tell you I'd *see you later*? We were standing beneath Ana Rupene's portrait—remember?'

She became indignant. 'I didn't know you'd bring me to this place. I'm not in the habit of making such appointments—nor am I in the habit of kissing men I hardly know.' The colour flooded into her face as she recalled the ardour and intensity of her own response to the pressure of his lips.

His tone took on a mocking quality. 'Then let me say—for an amateur—you did remarkably well. I've seldom been kissed in such a manner that's made me long for more.'

Her face burned. 'Now you're laughing at me,' she retorted heatedly. 'I can read your mind quite easily, Adam Malvern. You think I'm cheap. You think I'm an easy mark for your male needs. Well—*I'm not*.' She struggled to disengage herself from the arms that were still about her.

'Watch your step,' he warned, 'you might slip again. If you do I'll let you fall—rather than give you a repeat performance.' The words were flung at her tauntingly.

She almost choked with fury. 'Your masculine ego makes me feel *sick*,' she hissed coldly. 'No doubt you think I'm standing here just waiting for your kiss—but if you imagine I'm a—a diversion from—from someone else—you're very much mistaken.'

His eyes narrowed as he stared at her through the gloom of the cave. 'A diversion? What the hell are you talking about? What could possibly give you such an idea?'

'Huh! Don't you think I've heard about you—and Elaine?'

'What would you have possibly heard about Elaine and me?'

'Just what everyone says—that sooner or later you'll marry her. It's true—isn't it?'

'*They say!* So that is what *they* say?' he mocked. 'Who are *they*?'

'I asked you if it's true. I notice you didn't answer.'

'You may think so if it pleases you to do so.' He spoke quietly.

'But you've brought Elaine here,' she accused as though unable to control her tongue. 'I *know* you've brought her here.'

'Oh? How could you possibly know?'

'You can call it instinct. Besides—isn't this what she meant when she declared you'd show *me* all the interesting places you'd shown *her*?'

'It's possible. But there's something you're forgetting. Elaine is a local girl—dammit—I didn't have to show her this place. She has always known about it. Do you imagine this cave is unknown to the local people?' He was looking at her intently, almost as though seeing her for the first time. 'You know—you can be quite a little spitfire. One would almost imagine you to be—jealous.'

His words shocked her to her senses, causing her to

control her anger. She looked at him contritely. 'I'm sorry—I shouldn't have said those things. The fact that you've brought Elaine here is not my concern.'

'Yet you appear to be infuriated.'

'If you must know—I'm more angry with myself than with you.'

'Why? Is it because you revelled in being kissed by a man—but hate to admit it?'

She bristled. 'How dare you suggest I revel in being kissed by men? It's as I said—you think I'm cheap——'

'Perhaps that was a bit strong—but I know you enjoyed being kissed by this particular man.'

She was unable to find an answer, mainly because the accusation was true, and as she recalled those moments of ecstasy she felt a warm glow creeping over her body.

His voice vibrated through the gloom. 'Are you afraid to be honest, Julie? Or was that passionate response just one big damnable lie? Perhaps you're just a good little actress——'

Again she remained silent, fearing that whatever she said would betray the fact that she longed to feel his arms about her once more—that she was ready and willing to compete with Elaine. She took a deep breath, shocked by her own thoughts. Where was her pride? How did her emotions get into this tangle?

His voice became hard. 'I notice you're finding difficulty in admitting the truth—so perhaps honesty isn't one of your major characteristics. So many women are born liars—and if there's one thing that really disgusts me, it's dishonesty.'

'I think it's time you took me home,' she snapped at him coldly.

'You're damned right, it is.' He turned and stalked out of the cave leaving her to find her own way over the slippery ground.

They made their way down the hill in silence. He opened the car door for her, then took his place behind the wheel, his mouth tight, his dark brows drawn together. She kept her chin averted, even so she could see the gleam of his white knuckles as he gripped the steering wheel.

Bumping over the field towards the farm road he gritted, 'I suppose you'd prefer to go straight home to Molly.'

'Definitely. At least it'll rid you of my presence—one whom you consider to be dishonest.' Unshed tears stung her eyes.

'Actually I had intended taking you home to Lucy who'll be expecting me to bring you to have a cup of tea with her. She'll have had her rest and the tea will be ready at three-thirty.'

'Will she be disappointed if I don't come back with you?'

'Most disappointed. Anyone could see she enjoyed talking to you. It was kind of you to make the effort to cheer an old lady, and I'd like you to know I appreciated it.'

She gave a light laugh. 'Surely—you're exaggerating.'

'Indeed, I'm not. You brought her to life.'

'Well—let me assure you there was no effort attached to it. Lucy is easy to talk to—despite our *generation* gap. Nor does she impress me as being very old.'

'She's turned sixty.'

'Is that all? Well now—fancy that.' Her tone was scornful. 'That's not old by today's standards, although I know there are *old* sixties and *young* sixties. However, I suppose depression is inclined to make one appear to be older than one's actual years.'

'Depression? What are you talking about?'

Before she could answer he stopped the car and got out to open a gate. The pause while he drove through it, then closed it again, gave her the opportunity to think for several moments before answering his question. Should she tell him what she thought about Lucy's situation and the so-called secret ailment he'd referred to when discussing her with Molly? It was neither her

problem nor her business, Julie realised, but if
anything could be said to assist Lucy's peace of
mind—then let it be said. No doubt he'd be furious
with her, but what did that matter? She'd already
made him angry with her, so a little more wouldn't
make much difference. And—perhaps—it *could* help
Lucy.

As he took his seat behind the wheel once more he
sent her a sharp glance. 'Well—I'm waiting. What do
you mean by depression? Are you suggesting Lucy's
depressed?'

She took a deep breath before she said, 'If you want
me to be frank I think it's fairly obvious.'

'You're saying you think her trouble is mental rather
than a physical ailment of some sort?'

'Yes. I believe her trouble is—is insecurity coupled
with a deep fear of what the future may hold for her.'

He gave a laugh that echoed his derision. 'That's
utter rubbish. There's no need for her to feel insecure.
As for her future—she knows she can live at Malvern
for the rest of her life.'

'She does?' A smile touched Julie's soft lips. 'You're
sure of that?'

'Of course I'm sure. What you're saying is a lot of
humbug and entirely your own imagination.' His tone
was curt.

'I prefer to call it my observation. Don't you know
that an onlooker who casts a fresh eye over a situation
is often quick to see something that's been hidden from
those closest to it?'

He was silent as he got out to open another farm
gate, but when they were driving on again he said with
an edge to his voice, 'You probably think you're being
very smart. Could you also be clever enough to offer a
suggestion?'

'You could polish up your own observation,' she
smiled, conscious of an inward flow of satisfaction as
she realised her words had not fallen upon entirely deaf

ears. 'Unless it doesn't *suit* you to do so, of course,' she added as an afterthought.

'What's that supposed to mean?' he scowled.

'I'm afraid you'll have to work it out for yourself,' she retorted drily. 'No doubt Elaine will help you to see things in a clearer light——' She stopped suddenly, annoyed with herself. She hadn't meant to utter those last words but somehow they'd just slipped out. Nor were they without effect.

Adam stopped the car on the road winding through the fields and turned to face her. 'What the hell has this to do with Elaine?'

She sighed. 'Why are men so blind? Can't you see it for yourself—for Pete's sake?'

'*Dammit*—see what?'

She stared straight ahead. 'Adam—this discussion has gone much further than I intended. I don't want to say these things—but for Lucy's sake it might be better if I do. How long has she been with you?'

'Fifteen years. She came to us after my mother died. I was fifteen and I'm now thirty.' His mouth had thinned to a grim line as he waited for her to continue.

'So for all those years—until Elaine came—she ran the house? She was the homemaker?'

'Yes—I suppose so.'

'But when Elaine came the job was taken from her before she was ready to give it up. Or so it seems to me. And now the suggestion of a pensioner flat appears to have been brought forward.'

'Just a minute,' he snapped. 'I'd say your imagination is working overtime. At lunch, if I remember correctly, it was you who brought up the subject of pensioner flats. Elaine would hardly suggest that Lucy should go into such a place.'

'Wouldn't she? If you question Lucy I think you'll find it's been mentioned before today.' She became exasperated. 'Really—you men make me feel tired. You're all the same—arrogant—domineering—and full of your own opinions. Yet, when a plain situation lies right under your noses you're too dumb to see it.'

'An authority on men, are you, Julie?'

'Of course not—but it's difficult to miss some aspects of their characters, especially when many are so similar.'

He watched her narrowly. 'Do I detect a bitter note? I suspect you've had a recent experience with a man, something unpleasant that's given you a real jar. Come on—admit it.'

His accusation left her speechless until, prevaricating, she asked coldly, 'What on earth would give you such an idea?'

'The way you kissed me in the cave. Now I can see you weren't kissing me at all. You were kissing somebody else. Who is he?'

'Do you really think I'd tell you?' she murmured turning away to stare across the fields that undulated between valleys and hills.

'No. Nor have I the right to question you.'

'No right at all,' she agreed.

'Nevertheless I think I can guess the situation. You've had a serious quarrel with your boyfriend. You wanted to get away from him for a while, so you came to Molly and Ted. Am I right?'

She found difficulty in meeting his eyes. It was better to let him believe there was someone else, she decided. Strangely, until recently, there *had* been someone else. There had been Ross—but he was now a shadowy figure in the background. She hadn't loved him at all. Instead of being in love with the man she'd been in love with love, and the idea of being engaged.

The knowledge startled her and she began to wonder about Anna. Did Anna really love Ross, or was she going through the same stage of immaturity? Julie hoped not, and she found she could now sincerely hope that Anna and Ross would be happy.

Adam said, 'You haven't answered me, but your

ilence is all I need to tell me my guess is right.' He set
he car in motion and they continued along the twisting
arm road towards the homestead.

When they reached the house they found Elaine
bout to pour the tea while Lucy sat on a settee with a
ile of old photographs on her lap. It was easily seen
he'd been waiting for them to return, and she now
ndicated that Julie should sit beside her.

'I thought of these photos while I was having my
est,' she explained. 'I'm sure you'd like to see some of
hem. Now that's Adam when he was a baby—and
here he is as a three-year-old.'

Adam gave a snort of exasperation. 'Hell's teeth,
ucy, she'll be bored to tears with that load from the
ast.'

'She'll be interested,' Lucy asserted with calm
onfidence as she handed the photos to Julie. The
teady look in the brown eyes was one of complete
nderstanding, and it was almost as though she knew
ulie's heart had contracted as she gazed at the round-
aced, wide-eyed baby, and at the cherubic small boy.

'These photos will give you an idea of Malvern's
arly days,' Lucy continued. 'This slab shack with its
hingled roof was the first shelter to be built on this
and, and then came this better cottage. You can see it
ad two bedrooms and a lean-to kitchen, also a proper
rick chimney and a veranda in front.'

Elaine came to peer at the photos. 'Very comfortable,'
he commented dryly, then in a slightly aggrieved tone,
. notice you've never bothered to show these old
hotos to me, Lucy.'

'I didn't think you'd be interested.'

'You didn't? So what makes you think Julie's
nterested?' Elaine's tone had taken on an edge.

'Oh—well—Julie's different,' Lucy said complacently.

'*Different*——? Why is she different?' Elaine pursued
harply.

But Lucy ignored the question. Bending over a faded

print she said, 'In this photo you can see what the bush
was like. The trees were large and high with branches
meeting overhead—and this photo shows a bullock
team hauling a large trunk towards one of the sawmills.
I must say Adam is fortunate to possess these old
photos because they tell the story of the Malvern land.
They're history. Of course the bush had to be cleared
before the pastures could be sown.'

Elaine turned to Adam. 'Speaking of pastures—
weren't you going to examine the ones out at the back?
How did you find the ones up near the cave? I'm sure
you took Julie to the cave,' she drawled, her hazel eyes
wide as they rested upon him.

'Of course,' he replied blandly. 'Everyone has to see
the cave. It'd be unkind to keep Julie in the dark
concerning its existence.'

She turned to Julie. 'And Dixie and Dell—I'm sure he
introduced you to them.'

Julie shook her head. 'No—I didn't see them.'

Elaine's eyes narrowed. 'Are you saying he didn't
show you his precious brood mares? My goodness—
you *must* have spent a long time in the cave.'

It was difficult to meet the onslaught calmly, but
after taking a deep breath Julie said, 'Yes—we were
there for quite a time. It was a new experience for
me.' She forced herself to look directly at Adam and
was perturbed to find a mocking glint in his dark eyes.
It sent the blood racing through her veins, causing
her to lower her gaze to the next photo Lucy held
towards her.

'Ah—here we have a school photo,' the small woman
said. 'It's one taken of all the boys and girls in the class.
See—there's Adam. He must've been about twelve—
and there's Elaine sitting beside him.'

'And I'm still sitting beside him,' Elaine said archly,
her voice betraying a small note of triumph.

The remark was followed by a silence until Lucy
changed the subject. Turning to Adam she asked, 'Have

ou decided upon taking the ewes from the Jordan
state? Have they lambs at foot?'

'Yes to both questions. I'll buy them all.'

'And you'll also give Dixie and Dell a spell up on
Vhariti?' Lucy pursued.

'Yes. A couple of weeks on the slopes before they're
oo near their foaling time will be good for them.
ortunately I'm able to rent land up there, but before
loing so I'll examine the quality of the feed.'

'Nothing but the best for Dixie and Dell,' Elaine said
easingly.

Julie looked at her thoughtfully. Although the words
ıad been spoken in a joking manner she sensed an
ınderlying resentment behind them. It was almost as
hough Elaine had warned that any woman rash enough
o set her sights on Adam Malvern would find herself
•laying second fiddle to a horse. And this, her expression
eemed to say, was the cross she herself had to bear.

Lucy's voice startled Julie from her musings. 'Have
ou been up on Whariti yet? It's quite high at the top—
•ver three thousand feet.'

'No, I haven't been up there. The view must be
remendous.'

'It's mainly a panorama of hills. Perhaps Adam will
ake you with him when he goes to examine the
•astures.'

Julie sent a nervous glance towards Adam but found
erself unable to meet his eyes. After this afternoon's
pisode she doubted that he'd be anxious to take her
nywhere, nor did he echo anything in the way of an
ffirmative to Lucy's suggestion.

Instead he stood up and glanced at his watch as
hough hinting it was time for her departure. 'I presume
ou'd like to have another look at the pups before I
ake you home?' It was a command rather than a
uestion.

She rose to her feet hastily. 'Oh yes—please——'
hen she turned to say goodbye to Lucy.

Lucy clung to her hand. 'Promise you'll visit me again soon.'

'Yes—of course——'

Adam led her out to the shed where they were welcomed by Fay whose tail thumped the ground vigorously as she lay with her four pups, whose beautiful brown eyes shone as they squatted beside her on the fresh straw.

'The cuddly little darlings—I adore them,' Julie murmured as she nursed and crooned over each one before returning it to its mother. And as she replaced each pup Fay licked her hand.

'She's accepted you,' Adam remarked as she stood up, then his voice became low and deep as he said, 'How about giving me a little of the same treatment?' His arms went out to snatch her to him, holding her against his breast while his chin rested upon her smooth forehead, his quickened breath fanning her cheek.

The action startled her but she did not resist him, and as she leaned her head against his shoulder her pulses began to race.

'Put your arms around me,' he demanded.

Obediently, her arms crept about his neck and, as though she had no will to stem her own desires, her face was raised. His dark eyes looked intently into her own for several moments, and as her lids fluttered and closed she felt his lips trail across her brow and cheeks before their pressure rested upon her mouth.

'Julie—what devil sent you across my path?' he murmured huskily at last.

Her fingers fondled the hair at the back of his head, and even as she told herself that this was to be nothing more than a short sisterly caress his mouth descended again, his kiss deepening as he parted her lips. Again she was drawn up into the dizzy heights of ecstasy, her thumping heart sending the blood careering madly through her veins until suddenly it was as it had been in the cave.

Rapture gripped her and the control she'd vowed to retain disappeared like a small puff of smoke from a cigarette. She knew that the pressure of one hand in the small of her back was causing her to arch towards him while the other caressed her as it began to explore her body. It slipped beneath the light blue lacy top she wore with her skirt, and a small gasp escaped her as she felt his fingers cup her breast.

'Adam—no—stop it at once——' Her voice seemed strangled as she struggled to remove his hand.

'Stop——? I haven't even begun yet. Are you afraid I'll roll you in the hay?'

'You—you might think it's a good idea to try,' she gasped.

'Do you imagine you're about to be raped?'

'Is that what you have in mind?' she snapped furiously.

He stared at her searchingly. 'Perhaps you want me to stop because you'd rather I was somebody else?'

She looked at him wordlessly. Surely it was impossible for him to have heard about Ross. 'What are you talking about?' she managed to ask at last.

'Who is he?' he rasped.

'Who——?' She continued to stare at him blankly. 'Who—what do you mean?'

'This fellow you imagine you're kissing—what's his name?'

She shook her head, unable to find words until she whispered, 'There isn't anyone—not now——'

'Ah—but there was?'

She became angry. 'I'm telling you—*there isn't anyone.*'

'And I'm telling you I don't believe you. You're lying again, just as you did when I asked you your name. Okay—get in the car. I'll take you home.'

CHAPTER FIVE

ANGER came to Julie's assistance. Coupled with pride it enabled her to sit with her head held high as the Peugeot sped along the dusty country road. She knew that Adam shot several side glances towards her, but she had no intention of allowing him to know that deep within herself she was a weeping bundle of misery, that she longed to huddle against the seat and let the tears fall.

At last he said, 'You're very silent. Does this mean you're sulking? A long face doesn't suit you.'

'I never sulk,' she retorted furiously. 'I'm merely wondering.'

'Oh? Wondering about what?' Curiosity tinged his voice.

'Why you should be so uptight because you think I'm imagining—somebody else——'

He remained silent, staring at the road ahead.

'What is it to you? Why should you worry about who I think I'm kissing?' Forcing herself to look at him she saw that his mouth had tightened. *'It's not your business,'* she added, emphasising each word.

'No—it's not my business,' he agreed, 'except that I refuse to act as a stand-in for anyone.'

'Then kindly keep your hands off me. I didn't ask you to kiss me. It was your own idea.'

'Wrong. Body and soul—you're crying out to be loved. Don't you think I can sense it?'

'If you're suggesting I'm longing to be rolled in the hay—well—that's just another insult to add to the one of being dubbed a liar. Therefore, in future, I'd be grateful if you'd leave me alone. Just *don't touch me.'*

This, she decided firmly, would be the wisest plan. It

78

would prevent her from making a prize idiot of herself by clinging and responding with an ardour she was unable to control. That's if he *did* take her in his arms again, of course, although after her last words that prospect now seemed unlikely.

'As you wish. In future I'll ignore you.'

Saddened, she was jerked into realising that perhaps this would be for the best because startling fears were now creeping into her mind, the first being the knowledge that while Ross's kisses had left her feeling cool and calm, the pressure of Adam's lips on her own had set her blood on fire. Nor had she ever actually longed for the feel of Ross's arms about her—whereas the strength of Adam's embrace as he moulded her to his body sent quivers shooting through her entire being.

It was like an awakening—the sudden stepping from girlhood to womanhood. The trees and the golden fields of buttercups became a blur as she gazed at them unseeingly, while a new fear began to manifest itself within her mind. Despite the short time she'd known him she realised she was in danger of falling in love with this arrogant, domineering Malvern man.

The thought disturbed her to such an extent that she sat in silence for the rest of the drive home, hardly daring to glance at the handsome profile as he stared ahead. Nor did Adam offer any further comment until he opened the car door for her.

'How long do you intend staying here?' he inquired tersely.

The abrupt question surprised her. 'I don't know. I really haven't thought about it. Would you prefer that I leave at once?'

'Certainly not,' he snapped, annoyed by the suggestion. 'You're the guest of Ted and Molly. Your visit has nothing to do with me except for one fact. Lucy is sure to want me to bring you to see her again.'

'And that's something you'd prefer not to happen. Don't worry—I quite understand.'

'I doubt that you do. If she asks me to bring you I'd like you to come. I'm grateful for any small diversion that's likely to give her pleasure.'

'I'm glad you care about her,' she said quietly. 'I rather wondered—if you did.'

The dark brows drew together. 'What's that supposed to mean? Why the hell should you think I don't care about Lucy?'

'Because of the situation you've allowed to develop. However, I can understand it—if Elaine means something special to you.'

'Can you, indeed? Well—perhaps I've been a trifle blind. Elaine's a damned good housekeeper and I've been coasting along without noticing anything else. I'm pleased you've told me what you think and from now on I'll keep a closer eye on matters.'

'At least that's something,' Julie said. She was conscious of a warm glow spreading within her, although she was vitally aware that he'd failed to deny there was any special feeling between Elaine and himself.

She made a last effort. 'Adam—I'm sorry about that—that business concerning my name. Please believe me when I say I had every intention of telling you——'

'Oh yes?' He sent her a bleak look, then gave a slight shrug. 'After all—what does it matter?'

'It matters to me that you think I'm a liar,' she snapped.

He made no reply and she stood watching as he got into the car and drove away.

What does it matter? she thought bitterly. Nothing to him, apparently, but to her quite a lot. In fact—everything. Her heart was heavy as she entered the kitchen where she found Molly busily rolling pastry for an apple pie.

The plump woman smiled at her expectantly, then her expression changed as her shrewd blue eyes regarded Julie's face. 'What's the matter?' she asked anxiously. 'You look as if you've suddenly grown older. Is everything all right?'

Julie shook her head as she made an effort to control the tears that sprang unbidden to her eyes. 'Adam and I quarrelled. He's disgusted with me because he thinks I'm all the things he despises—dishonest, deceitful—a liar.'

'Rubbish. He can't possibly think that about you.' Molly lifted the pastry and laid it across the top of a dish filled with sliced Granny Smith apples. 'Does it matter?' she asked. 'I mean—do you care what Adam Malvern thinks about you?'

Julie had to be honest. 'Yes—I do. I care very much about what he thinks.' Her voice trembled slightly as she made the admission.

'Yet—wasn't it only yesterday that you cared very much about what somebody else thought?'

'Are you referring to Ross Mitchell?'

'I believe that's his name.'

'How did you know about that situation? I didn't tell you.'

Molly trimmed the overhanging pastry from the edge of the dish. 'I've been speaking to your mother on the phone. She rang to make sure you'd arrived here safely and that you weren't still down in the dumps. She told me you were upset when you left home, and she also told me what had put you into this state of depression. It must have been a shock.'

Julie nodded. 'I thought I'd die when Father said he'd given his permission for them to become engaged.'

'I can understand how much you wanted to get away from the sight of them being together. I'm glad you came to me although I did suspect there was a reason for your sudden visit. I've missed you and Anna—and of course your mother.'

'We missed you, too, Molly. We wept for ages when you left.'

'Really? I can just see your father wiping his eyes—I

don't think. But getting back to Anna—it's difficult to think of her being engaged to be married. She was always so much younger than her years—like a spoilt baby that had to have every whim satisfied. Has she changed?

'If she has, I haven't noticed it,' Julie answered truthfully.

'I just hope this Ross Mitchell fellow can give her all she demands because I doubt that she'll ever change her ways, and if I remember correctly she used to demand plenty.' She paused while she placed the pie in the oven, then, 'Well now—what about you? Are you getting him out of your mind?'

'Yes. I've already discovered I was never really in love with him. Since being here I've given him hardly a thought.'

Molly smiled. 'Don't you mean that since meeting Adam you've given him hardly a thought?'

Julie felt her colour rising. 'Well—yes—I'll admit he's helped to make me realise I didn't love Ross.'

Molly's round face became serious. 'Don't let him catch you on the rebound. It'd be easy for him to sweep you off your feet. Now then—I think you should phone your mother to assure her you're not moping over Anna's fiancé. Let her know you're not in the doldrums.'

'But I *am* in the doldrums, Adam thinks I'm a liar.'

'Forget Adam,' Molly advised tersely. 'Speak to Anna and let her tell you what her ring is like. There's the phone over on the bench. Go and use it.'

When Julie spoke to her mother she made an effort to force some brightness into her voice; nevertheless she found herself being chided for not having rung sooner.

'I was worried about you, dear,' Claire Forsyth said. 'You weren't in a fit state of mind to be driving through that Gorge—and going too fast, I'm sure.'

Julie waved her mother's fears aside. 'You can stop worrying about any state of mind I might've had about

Ross, Mother,' she assured her parent, then went on to tell her about Tim's trouble with boils. 'I'm riding Gallant and Cloud,' she explained, 'and I'll stay here until Ted no longer needs me.' She paused before asking anxiously, 'How's Father? Is he mad with me for coming here?'

'Not at all, dear. He had an appointment with the optometrist the day you went to Woodville, and since then he's been busy trying to adjust himself to his new contact lenses. Heaven alone knows why the man advised him to try them.'

'I can't imagine Father without his glasses, nor can I imagine him fiddling with contact lenses. He's far too impatient.'

'He's doing his best to become used to them. Personally I suspect it's vanity. He feels and looks younger without his glasses.'

Julie's mind switched to her sister. 'How is Anna? Is she still on top of the world? What is her engagement ring like?'

'She can tell you herself. Really—I can't understand her.' Clair's voice had taken on a sudden crispness.

Julie frowned, puzzled by her mother's tone, but the reason became clear when Anna came on the line.

'You were *mean* to me, Julie,' she complained in petulant tones. 'I asked you to come with us to help choose the ring—but you wouldn't.'

'Of course not. I don't go about choosing rings for other people. What's the matter with you, Anna?'

'I—I didn't get the one I wanted.'

'Oh? What did you get?'

'It's a cluster. It's quite nice, I suppose, but it's not the one I really wanted.'

'Which was——?'

'A gorgeous big solitaire. You should've seen it. *Beautiful.*'

'It's price tag being beautiful as well, I suppose? I'll bet it cost the earth.'

'Well—it cost a few thousand dollars, but don't you see—it would've proved he *loves* me. Now if you'd been there you could've persuaded Ross to buy it for me.'

Julie was appalled by the suggestion. 'You've got to be joking. That's the last thing I'd do. What did he say when you showed him the one you wanted?'

'He said I could have the solitaire if I wanted it.'

'He *did*? So why didn't you get it?'

'Because he also said he'd set aside a certain sum for a ring, and if I wanted one that cost more I'd have to pay the balance myself. *Can you imagine it?*' Anna's voice rang with indignation.

Julie began to laugh as her mind conjured up the vision of a mutinous Ross and a sulky Anna in the jeweller's shop. The scene struck her as being extremely funny and her giggles floated over the line to her sister's ear.

'Don't you dare laugh,' Anna shrilled as Julie's mirth reached her. 'It's all your fault——'

'Don't be stupid, Anna—it's time you grew up,' Julie snapped angrily. 'You can't expect Ross to run himself into debt just to satisfy your silly vanity.'

'You don't *understand*——' The receiver was slammed down.

Julie hung up and turned to Molly. 'You knew about this disappointment over the ring?'

Molly nodded. 'Your mother told me. She's upset by Anna's attitude. She fears it's a very poor beginning to their engagement and she can't help wondering how long it'll last. Ross isn't seeing Anna in a very good light, so he might be having second thoughts about her.' She looked at Julie thoughtfully. 'Are you sure you've got him right out of your system? If he's still lingering in it I'd say it's only a matter of time——'

Julie shook her head. 'Oh no—I told you—the feeling I had for Ross wasn't love. I—I realise that now.

'What you feel for Adam is—different?' Molly asked gently.

Julie flushed. 'Entirely different. It's something I've never known before. I can't understand how it could hit me from out of the blue like this, nor can I explain it.'

'Then don't try,' Molly advised. 'Just live with it and think about it very carefully. Perhaps it's just a passing infatuation.'

'Whatever it is, it gives me a pain. It's something deep down inside my chest, churning around until it hurts. Perhaps I should go home. I know I ran from home, but the sight of Anna and Ross together will no longer affect me in any way.'

Molly sighed. 'Ted won't be pleased to see you go. He's hoping you'll stay and ride for him until Tim's back on the job. The poor lad's having real trouble with this boil. It's when they're on a muscle that they really hurt, and now he's got a second one coming.'

'Of course I'll stay for as long as Ted needs me,' Julie assured her. Then, after a few moments' thought, 'Shouldn't Tim be having injections of some sort for his boils? I've heard they are a great help in getting rid of them.'

'Ted's taking him to the doctor in Woodville tomorrow morning,' Molly said. 'I thought we'd go with them and buy some stores. I've made a list of things I need.'

Julie nodded absently. She didn't care where she went or what she did, so long as occupation of some kind kept Adam's face from her mind. 'Please give me some jobs to do,' she pleaded.

That night she slept badly, turning from one side to the other as she wondered why fate had sent the Malvern man to cross her path. And even when she did sleep he strode about in her dreams, reaching out to touch her hand, then turning away before she could feel his clasp, frustrating her to such an extent it was a relief to hear the sound of the alarm at daybreak.

She sprang out of bed and dressed hastily before joining Ted and Tim in the kitchen where tea and toast

had been made. It was all gulped down quickly, and a
short time later she was on her way to the racecourse to
give Gallant and Cloud their pacework.

Ted was delighted to see her handle the horses so
easily. 'You'll be paid for all this good work,' he
promised as he legged her up into the exercise saddle on
Gallant's back.

She laughed, brushing the suggestion aside. 'Give it
to Tim,' she suggested generously. 'His need's greater
than mine.'

But Ted was serious. 'The boss would have to pay
somebody else if you weren't here,' he pointed out.

She felt her colour rising. 'Huh! Take money from
him? Not likely. I couldn't bear it. Perhaps you could
look upon it as payment for my board and lodging,' she
told him loftily.

Ted's sharp eyes squinted up at her. 'Like that, is it? I
reckon you're getting keen on him. You just watch it,
young Julie, I don't want to see you hurt in any way.'

She forced a smile. 'Don't worry about me, Ted. I
can steer my own emotions.'

'Good girl—just make sure you keep a tight rein on
them.'

Riding work followed the pattern of the previous
morning. The horses behaved well, settling down to
their required pacework on the plough. The same
groups of boys were there, following a similar training
programme with their thoroughbreds and shouting
their jocular remarks if they happened to draw near to
Julie.

And although it was exhilarating to breathe in the
fresh morning air, to feel the glow of the early sun on
her face, all was not perfect because the sight of Adam
watching her from the rail was missing.

She had fully expected him to be there, and her eyes
constantly scanned the circumference of the course for
the sight of his tall figure, but there was no sign of him.
His absence depressed her, and it was with something of

a shock that she became aware of how much his presence meant to her.

A gloomy sense of dejection wrapped itself about her as she put first Cloud and then Gallant through their pacework, and she was almost glad when both horses had been hosed down at the end of their morning session.

On the journey back to the stables she rode Cloud while leading Gallant, arriving home to find Molly with breakfast ready and Tim waiting to feed the horses. A hot bath soothed and helped to remove her despondency, and by the time they left to take Tim to the doctor her spirits had risen.

Ted's Holden took only a few minutes to cover the short distance to the Woodville township where the few shops lay on either side of the main highway. He stopped near the Lindauer restaurant to allow Molly and Julie to get out of the car, then he continued to the doctor with Tim.

'There aren't many shops but they offer most of what we need,' Molly said as she led Julie into an antique and second-hand shop where she loved to browse among the large array of china plates.

But Julie was more interested in the extensive display of riding equipment in the saddler's shop across the road. For such a small town the variety of stock was surprising, she thought, until she recalled that Ted had told her there were almost twenty thoroughbred training stables within the vicinity of Woodville.

They looked in every shop on both sides of the business area until they came to the main general store where Molly consulted her list for the groceries she needed. Julie then decided to retrace her steps to a bookshop for some magazines, and she was making her way back to the general store when she saw Adam and Elaine leave an office doorway across the road.

Elaine was eye-catching in a high-collared straight dress of deep red that seemed to complement her black hair. A matching jacket turned the outfit into a suit, while the black bag swinging from her shoulder matched her black high-heeled sandals.

Looking at her Julie felt herself to be dull and uninteresting in her full-skirted dove-grey dress with its pink trim which Mother had declared to be so *suitable* because it wasn't *loud*—but which now made her feel like a fourth-form teenager. She hastened her steps towards the store, hoping to escape before they saw her, but they had already begun to cross the road.

Elaine's voice came to her ears. 'Hi—Julie—what's your hurry?' Her eyes rested on the magazines. 'You're buying reading matter? Are you becoming bored with life on this side of the Gorge?' Her tone was taunting.

Julie refused to be needled. 'On the contrary, life's very pleasant here,' she smiled. Her eyes turned to Adam, dragged in his direction as though by a magnet. 'You weren't at the course this morning. I expected you to be keeping an eye on the pacework Gallant and Cloud were being given.'

'I've learnt to respect Ted's judgment with regard to their handling,' he retorted abruptly. 'In any case I had another job on hand. I went up to Whariti to examine the pastures.'

'Oh.' Her voice echoed her dejection.

Elaine said lightly, 'I believe you're disappointed. Is it because Lucy said something about Adam taking you up there? I can assure you he's far too busy to be running round after people, although today he's actually taking a couple of hours off——'

Adam cut into her words. 'Where's Ted?' he demanded of Julie. 'In town? I meant to call in on the way here——'

'He's taken Tim to the doctor,' Julie told him.

'Right. When you see him please give him a message. Tell him Dixie and Dell are to go up top this afternoon.'

Elaine became impatient. 'Must we waste time

standing here?' she complained, looking up into Adam's face. 'You know you promised to take me to see the canoe-racing in the Gorge.' She sent a look of thinly veiled triumph towards Julie. 'We're taking fish and chips from the Lindauer so it'll be like a picnic. Sorry you can't join us.' A brittle laugh followed her last words.

'Goodbye,' Julie said quietly. She looked at Adam, expecting a comment from him but his mouth had thinned to a tight line and he said nothing.

They moved away from her, walking along the pavement beneath the continuous stretch of veranda roofing that sheltered the shop windows from the glare of the sun or from rainstorms. An inability to move possessed her, and as she watched their departing backs she stared hard at the tall figure of Adam, concentrating upon him and doing her best to will him to pause and look back at her. But it was useless. He gave not even the briefest glance over his shoulder.

Molly's voice brought her to her senses. 'Are you rooted to the spot? I've spoken to you three times.'

'I—I saw Adam—he's with Elaine,' she admitted dolefully. 'They came out of that doorway across the road.'

Molly glanced in the direction Julie indicated. 'That's nothing unusual. It's his accountant's office. He's probably been there on business, either for himself or on behalf of Elaine's mother. Didn't I tell you their parents were old friends? Since the death of her husband a couple of years ago Elaine's mother has had a young man running the farm for her, but an arrangement was made for Adam to act as an overseer. He keeps an eye on the accounts, the stock replacements and general maintenance of the place. It's a pity Elaine didn't have a brother, but she's an only child.'

Julie's mind leapt towards the future. 'Therefore, if Adam marries her his children will inherit not only his property but also the farm that now belongs to her mother?'

'Yes, I suppose so.' Molly looked at her sharply. 'I've already warned you that people who know them are expecting to hear wedding bells sooner or later, so if you're developing any serious feelings for Adam this is something you really must remember.'

Julie avoided discussing the depth of her feelings for Adam. It was difficult enough trying not to look too closely at them herself, and although she told herself it was infatuation and that it would pass, she knew that such was not the case. At last she said, 'I wonder why they're taking so long about getting married.'

Molly shook her head vaguely. 'Who can tell? Perhaps he's undecided about his feelings towards her, but I can assure you that when he does make a commitment, that woman—whoever she happens to be—will certainly know he loves her.'

'What makes you so positive?' Julie asked in a low voice.

'Because he never does anything by halves.'

They went back into the shop where they browsed among an array of crockery, hardware and clothing until they saw the Holden being parked near the entrance. The trolley laden with Molly's purchases was then pushed out to the kerbside, and as Ted unloaded it into the boot Julie gave him the message concerning the two brood mares.

Molly glanced at her watch. 'Goodness—it's nearly one o'clock. Isn't it time we had lunch? Let's take fish and chips home from the Lindauer.' She looked at Ted, awaiting his approval.

'Tim shouldn't be eating fish and chips,' he demurred. 'He's supposed to be keeping his weight down.'

There was an instant protest from Tim. 'Aw—gee, Boss—I'm on sick leave today—it's ages since I had fish and chips——'

'Okay—you can have them today,' Ted yielded reluctantly.

Julie said nothing. She knew fish and chips would be the last type of food she'd enjoy while her mind was filled with thoughts of Adam and Elaine dipping into similar packets of hot potatoes and tasty batter-covered cod or groper.

Where were they now? she wondered. Probably in the picnic area near the entrance to the Gorge. No doubt they were watching the canoeists preparing to cope with the deep narrow waters that rushed between the gap in the two mountain ranges. A sudden bitterness filled her, stinging her eyes with unshed tears that had to be blinked away, and she knew she was jealous. Yes— *jealous*, she admitted to herself.

The Lindauer restaurant was on a corner a short distance along the road, and while Ted went into the takeaway-food department the others waited in the car. They sat watching the traffic make its way along the main street of Woodville, but Julie's mind was so obsessed by thoughts of Adam and Elaine that she hardly saw it.

Suddenly she found herself saying, 'Adam and Elaine have gone to watch the canoe-racing in the Gorge.' It was almost as though the words had been dragged from her, heaping coals on the fire of her inner torture. Then, annoyed with herself for having mentioned the two names uppermost in her mind, she made a desperate attempt to change the subject. Turning to Tim she said, 'Do you know about the Manawatu river, Tim? It's really quite unique.'

He looked blank. 'Oh? What's unique about it? It's only a moving strip of water, isn't it?'

'Well—I suppose it's only a hundred miles long, but it's unique because it rises on one side of a main dividing range and flows into the sea on the opposite side of the same range. It does that by twisting round and cutting through the Gorge,' she added.

'Heaven alone knows how it ever cut through the range,' Molly said. 'Even the geologists are still puzzled about the way it happened.'

'But not the Maori people,' Julie laughed. 'According to their legends a giant totara tree on this side of the range decided it wanted to go to the coast, so it wrenched itself up from where it was growing on the mountainside, flung itself down into a gully and smashed a path through the range while making its way to the sea.'

They were still laughing over the improbability of this story when Ted returned to the car, his arms full of parcels which he handed round. As he got into the car Tim leaned forward eagerly.

'Say—what d'ye know, Boss—there's canoe-racing in the Gorge. Couldn't we have five minutes dekko at it?' he pleaded.

Ted scowled. 'Those idiots are welcome to drown themselves if they want to, Tim. As for us—we've got a special job to do.'

'Aw—gee—not even just five lousy minutes——?'

Ted capitulated. 'Okay, just five minutes—but no more.'

Molly looked at Ted as they drove along the highway towards the Gorge. 'What special job has to be done?' she asked.

'The boss wants Dixie and Dell taken up to Whariti. When we get home we'll hitch the horse trailer to the truck, collect them from their home paddock and take them up there.'

'It's very steep country,' Molly reminded him doubtfully.

'It'll give them good pre-foaling exercise,' Ted pointed out.

Julie was too disappointed to utter a word. Hadn't Lucy suggested that Adam should take her with him when he went up to examine the Whariti pastures? Apparently he'd had no wish to do so. Even Elaine had recalled the suggestion——.

Molly turned curious eyes upon Ted. 'When did Adam ask you to do this? The phone didn't ring and he hasn't been to the house.'

'He came to the racecourse this morning and told me he was going up to look at the feed on Whariti, and then he left a message with Julie when he saw her in the street.'

'I didn't see him at the racecourse,' Julie exclaimed, unable to remain silent any longer.

'Well—he was there,' Ted assured her. 'I was hosing down Cloud when he came to the stalls.' He caught her eye in the rear vision mirror. 'Are you saying he didn't go over to the plough to watch Gallant doing his pacework?'

Pride came to her rescue. 'I was probably concentrating so hard on keeping Gallant at the right speed that I—I didn't notice him.' It was difficult to keep the misery out of her voice.

'Eat your fish and chips while they're hot,' Molly advised, almost as though she sensed Julie's need for a diversion from thoughts that were anything but happy.

Reluctantly, she tore a hole in the top of the packet, pulled out a chip and nibbled at it.

Tim watched her slow progress with interest. 'If you don't like 'em I'll eat any you don't want,' he offered hopefully.

'No you won't, young Tim,' Ted said sternly over his shoulder.

The road wound towards the ranges until the riverflats spreading below them on the left formed a suitable starting place for the canoe-racing. A gateway near the road gave access. Ted drove through it, then continued down the hill to where a tree-sheltered picnic area lay below the level of the road. Several cars were already parked in it, their trailers still bearing small watercraft of various types.

Further along the river a break in the mountain range formed the eastern portals of the Gorge. The river swept through them, and as the suddenly narrowed waters rushed between the boulder-lined banks they gathered speed until they reached the western opening four miles away.

'It's a tricky course for those little canoes,' Ted observed as he dipped into his packet of fish and chips.

They remained seated in the car watching people enjoy their picnic lunches or wander among the variety of canoes and kayaks, and although the green Peugeot was parked only a short distance away they could see no sign of Adam or Elaine until Tim uttered a sudden squeak of excitement.

'Blimey—will you take a dekko at that lot. It's the boss—*nursing his girl in broad daylight.*'

It was indeed Adam and Elaine. He carried her in his arms towards the Peugeot.

'Do you think she's had an accident? Perhaps she's hurt her ankle—or something.' Molly cast an anxious glance towards Julie.

Ted snorted disdainfully. 'I doubt it. See how she smiles as she clings to him. She's not in any pain—that's for sure.'

'Perhaps she's pinned him down at last,' Tim whispered, his voice full of suppressed excitement.

Julie said nothing. She felt herself gripped by an icy chill as she watched their progress towards the car. Elaine's arms were entwined round Adam's neck, she noticed—just as her own had been—and little effort was needed to imagine the rapt expression on her face as she gazed up into his eyes.

Yet it was only yesterday when Adam had held Julie in his arms. He'd kissed her passionately as his hands had moulded her body against his own, and the memory of it made her feel physically ill. She turned away to stare unseeingly up the river and towards the distant hills. The sight of Elaine being carried by Adam was almost more than she could bear.

CHAPTER SIX

Tim's voice, breathless with anticipation, came to Julie's ears. 'Look—he's setting her feet down on the ground near the Peugeot. I wonder why he was carrying her. She's not limping nor nothing like that——'

'You can ask him when he gets here—if you dare,' Ted commented drily. 'They're coming this way now.'

Julie forced herself to turn her head and observe the approaching couple, fully expecting them to be walking arm in arm, but, to her surprise, such was not the case. Adam strode along briskly while Elaine's high heels caused difficulty in keeping up with him.

'Hello there——' Ted greeted them affably as they reached the Holden. 'Having trouble of some sort?'

Adam's dark brows rose. 'Trouble? I don't think so.'

Ted grinned. 'I mean—you seemed to find it necessary to carry the lady,' he pointed out bluntly.

Elaine laughed. 'Oh—*that*. Wasn't it sweet of him? He was saving my expensive Italian sandals. Well—it was his fault. He insisted upon walking along the riverbank to have a closer look at those high walls of bush across the water. And what happened? We got into a boggy patch and I couldn't move without ruining my very best sandals, so I just stood still and told him he'd either carry me back to the car or I'd stay there for evermore.'

'Can you imagine the shrieks and screams if I'd walked off and left her stuck in the mud?' Adam asked grimly. 'It was much easier to carry her back than to have a scene.'

Elaine's hazel eyes held a glint of triumph as they rested upon Julie. 'Have they brought you to see the canoe-racing? If so I'm afraid you'll have to wait for some time yet because the races have been delayed. Several of the contestants are late in arriving.'

'In that case we'll leave,' Ted declared with finality. 'I'm not sitting here for another hour or more while those two mares are waiting to be moved up to Whariti.'

'You're right—it'd be ridiculous,' Adam agreed. 'I'll come and give you a hand with them.'

There was an instant protest from Elaine. 'Oh no— we'll miss the canoe-racing. I want to see the kayaks in the rapids——'

'The mares are more important than canoes or kayaks,' Adam told her bluntly and without a sign of regret. He turned to Tim who was sitting beside Julie in the back of the Holden. 'How are you, Tim? What did the doctor say?'

The apprentice jockey leaned forward and spoke politely. 'He gave me a jab and a prescription for some pills, Mr Malvern—sir. He doesn't want me to ride for several days, or at least a week.'

'We're damned lucky to have Julie with us,' Ted reminded Adam.

'Yes indeed—we are.' The words came crisply.

Julie knew the dark eyes were resting upon her but she refused to look at him; instead her chin rose slightly as she again turned her gaze up the river and towards the hills until at last she felt his scrutiny had left her.

'I'll meet you at the homestead,' Adam said to Ted. 'You and I can manage Dixie and Dell.' Then, favouring Molly and Julie with brief nods he made his way back to the Peugeot.

They sat watching Elaine teetering on her high heels as she followed him, the sight bringing an exasperated sigh from Molly. 'Stupid girl,' she said crossly. 'Fancy wearing expensive Italian sandals to the riverbank. I can hardly afford the best New Zealand-made sandals. He must pay her a good salary——'

Julie said nothing. There'd been no mention of her going up to Whariti, she noticed despondently, and if it weren't for Tim's indisposition and her promise to ride for Ted she'd pack up and go home immediately. Or would she? she wondered with honesty.

She did not see Adam during the following week. She rose at dawn each morning to give Gallant and Cloud their pacework, and each afternoon she walked the two thoroughbreds along the grassy verges of the quiet country backroads.

Ted always accompanied her to the racecourse for the pacework, and although her eyes constantly scanned the rails surrounding the large oval, she saw no sign of the tall owner of the Malvern stables. Nor did she meet him during any of her afternoon walks.

The rest of each day was spent helping Molly, and as her assistance halved the work their minds turned towards summer clothing.

'I really need something new,' Molly complained, staring into her wardrobe.

'I could run up a couple of dresses for you,' Julie offered.

Molly beamed. 'You *could*? That'd be wonderful.'

The next afternoon Ted walked the horses while Julie drove her red Fiat through the Gorge to Palmerston North where Molly chose light fabrics and patterns. On their return Molly's Bernina sewing-machine was lifted from its place of concealment at the bottom of the linen-cupboard and placed on a table in the small porch that led off from the kitchen.

Molly's eyes widened as she watched the efficiency with which Julie spread the materials on the carpet, then knelt to place the patterns and cut the fabrics. 'You've certainly got plenty of confidence with those scissors,' she exclaimed.

Julie smiled. 'I learnt to sew after you and Ted left. Do you remember how very much I wanted to become a vet?'

'Yes. You were always nursing an animal of some kind.'

'Well—I changed my mind and took a sewing course instead. Now then—I'd better check all your measurements again——'

The subject had been deliberately changed. There was no need to explain that after Ted and Molly had left Father had insisted she stayed home to help her mother, and that Mother had arranged for her to take the sewing course. It had really been something to keep her mind occupied and away from the disappointment of not being able to study veterinary science.

It was strange how the departure of Molly and Ted had changed her own plans, and how, through their leaving, she had now met Adam Malvern. Where was he? she wondered. Why didn't he come to see Gallant and Cloud? Had he visited the stables without her knowledge? Did this mean he was avoiding her for some reason? The questions twirled through her mind as she bent over the sewing-machine.

By the end of the week Molly had two new dresses styled to suit her plump figure. The making of them had helped to keep Julie's thoughts from straying towards Adam, and had kept at bay the constant nagging desire to see him. And then one afternoon when she had almost ceased to listen for his steps she received an unexpected surprise.

Sitting in the porch which had now become known as the sewing-room she was busily whipping round the hem of the second dress when she looked up to find him regarding her from the kitchen. He had come in unheard, and his sudden appearance caused her to catch her breath and sent the blood rushing to her face.

They stared at each other in silence for several moments, his dark eyes holding an intangible expression until they moved towards the array of sewing. She knew it puzzled him, but she made no attempt to enlighten him.

At last he said, 'Attending to your summer wardrobe? I'd have thought Miss Forsyth would've just gone out and bought whatever she desired.'

Refusing to be needled she forced herself to smile at him. 'May I ask what makes you an authority on my normal habits, Mr Malvern?'

'I understand that very few girls are capable of sewing these days. So many wear jeans instead of dresses.'

'Please don't judge me by—by the majority of your female friends. I enjoy sewing.' She snipped the thread and placed the dress on a hanger beside the first one she'd completed. 'I suppose you're looking for Ted. I think he's over at the stables—and Molly's outside picking flowers,' she added inconsequently.

'No, she's not,' Molly claimed as she came into the kitchen, her arms laden with a colourful bouquet of bright yellow forsythia and red, blue, mauve and white anemones. 'Ted's due in for his smoko if you're looking for him.'

'At the moment I'm looking at Julie's new dresses. These plain tailored lines are really smart.'

Molly laughed. 'Can't you see that those dresses are much too large for Julie? She's made them for me. Isn't she clever? Just look at the buttonholes and at the inside finish. It's really quite professional.'

'I'll admit I'm impressed,' he remarked drily. 'Do you accomplish everything else as well as you ride and sew?' His tone had become faintly sardonic.

'And as well as I tell lies?' she drawled. 'Apparently it pleases you to be sarcastic.'

Molly looked at Adam. 'Are you still annoyed because Julie didn't tell you her name? A girl meeting a stranger on the road isn't obliged to tell him her name—even if he does happen to be Adam Malvern. Ah—here's Ted. I'll make the tea.'

The men sat at the table, their discussion following its usual course by revolving round the horses. Cloud was due to run in a race the following Saturday—but was she ready for the race? Or should she be scratched from it?

Ted said, 'Julie's been giving her some fast work—but is it enough? Mind you, a run would be good for her. It'd be part of her education—keep in her mind what racing's all about.'

Adam said, 'There'll be a jockey at the course who'll mount her. There are always boys looking for extra rides.'

Julie had remained in the sewing-room because she had no wish to sit where she could see Adam, yet know herself to be ignored. It was enough to hear the resonant tones of his deep voice, and, listening to what was almost becoming an argument, she realised that while Adam was keen for Cloud to race, Ted was against it.

At last she went into the kitchen to fetch the cup of tea Molly had poured for her, and as she was about to carry it back to the sewing-room Ted put out a detaining hand. 'You've been riding Cloud, Julie,' he said. 'Do you think we should run her on Saturday? She'll have some stiff opposition.'

She thought for a moment, then spoke directly to Adam as she answered Ted's question. 'Do you consider it would be *honest*? You *know* she's not ready and that she's unlikely to win. Therefore would it be *fair* to the betting public—or would it be *deception*? I'd be most interested to hear your analysis of *honesty*, *lies* and deception in *this* particular case—Mr Malvern.' Then, knowing she had scored, and without waiting for his reply, she carried her tea back to her sunny corner in the sewing-room.

A long silence followed her departure from the room, but suddenly it was broken by the loud ringing of the telephone. Molly answered it, then called towards the sewing-room, 'It's for you——'

Surprised, Julie put down her cup. Perhaps it was

Mother wanting to know when she'd be coming home. Or Father—demanding her return. Or it could be Anna who had already rung twice about the alterations she was determined to have made to Ross's house. She had various projects in mind and what would Julie think about this latest idea? And why didn't she come home to help her decide?

Molly held the receiver towards her as she walked into the kitchen. 'It's a *man*,' she informed her with a grin.

Julie hesitated. 'A man—for me? Are you sure?'

'Of course I'm sure. He asked for you in a very polite manner.'

She took the receiver doubtfully. 'Hullo——?'

'Is that you, Julie? Gosh—do I need to talk to you——'

The familiarity of the voice struck her at once. Her face went scarlet as she said, 'Ross——? Is that you?'

'Of course it's me. I say—I've got to talk to you.'

'To me? Why? What about?'

'About a number of things. I'm in trouble and you're the only one who can help me.'

'What sort of trouble?'

'Well—it's Anna. I'm unable to cope with her.'

She gave a short laugh. 'Is this something you've just found out? I mean—you've known Anna for ages.'

'I'm beginning to wonder if I've ever known her.'

'Well—what's the matter?'

'The most important thing is—no—I refuse to discuss it over the phone. I say—is there anyone in the room listening?'

'Yes. At least three people.' She now felt fully composed.

'Look—I must meet you somewhere. I want to talk to you in private. Can I take you to dinner in Woodville?'

'There's a restaurant on the corner of the main highway. It's called the Lindauer.'

'Will you meet me there at seven-thirty this evening?'

She hesitated, having no wish to spend time over an evening meal with Ross, yet there was an urgency about his request. But perhaps it was the fact that Adam was listening which made her say, 'Yes—I'll be there at seven-thirty. Does Anna know about this—this talk you're so anxious to have with me?'

'Not at the moment. Later, perhaps. Please don't mention it if you happen to be speaking to her on the phone.'

'Very well. I must say I'm curious.' She replaced the receiver, then turned to find three pairs of eyes regarding her.

Ted said, 'So are we all curious. You mentioned Ross. Isn't he Anna's future husband? What does he want?'

'I've no idea,' Julie answered with truth, her brow creased in a troubled frown. 'I only know he wants to talk to me in private. Perhaps it's nothing important.'

'Or perhaps he wants to admit he's backed the wrong filly,' Ted prophesied shrewdly.

Julie was startled by the suggestion, then gave a small laugh to make light of the matter. 'You must have your little joke, Ted.' At the same time she became aware that Adam watched her closely.

Molly put in a sharp word. 'One thing's for sure, Ted. It's not our business.'

Whereupon Ted took the hint and nothing more was said concerning Julie's dinner date with her sister's fiancé.

Dressing to meet Ross that evening filled her with a strange sensation. The warm tan trouser-suit she put on was one she'd worn when she'd gone out with him during the winter, and it was like taking a step backwards into the past. But now, instead of the rising excitement of those days, she was conscious of little more than her earlier curiosity.

Why did he wish to talk to her? She felt sure it was

something to do with Anna. The whole situation was most peculiar, and for some unknown reason she became aware of a growing apprehension. Was Ted right in his surmise? Did Ross want to tell her he'd made a mistake? The fear grew stronger as she drove her red Fiat towards Woodville.

She reached the town at seven-thirty as requested, but there was no sign of Ross's Rover. The short length of the shopping-area was almost deserted and she had no option but to park outside the restaurant and wait for him. Towards the west she could see the dim outline of the hills against the evening sky, but this became blurred by the dazzle of car headlights coming from the direction of the Gorge.

Although she knew that at any moment one of the cars would be driven by Ross she felt no enthusiasm at the prospect of seeing him again. It's gone, she thought. The love I imagined I had for him has completely vanished. It's been killed by that—that Malvern man.

She waited almost fifteen minutes before the Rover pulled up on the opposite side of the highway. Ross got out, locked the car and strode across the road towards her. 'It's good to see you, Julie,' he exclaimed. 'Gosh—I've missed you.' He moved to take her in his arms but she evaded him. 'Come on——' he pleaded, 'you've kissed me before——'

She kept her voice cool. 'As you say—that was *before*.'

'Okay,' he muttered crossly. 'Let's go in and order food. I broke speed limits getting here—and I'm starving.'

They entered the small restaurant which was already half full of diners. A waitress led them to a table for two, presented them with menus, and after making a choice Julie looked about her with interest. So this was where Elaine had waited in vain for Adam during the evening Fay had had her pups.

The place was cosy and had an atmosphere of earlier

days which had been achieved by its fireplace of large river stones and the framed Lindauer portraits of Maori chiefs looking down from the walls. The place mats on the tables showed a photo of the artist's kindly intelligent face and gave a brief history of his life in New Zealand. Julie read every word concerning him until Ross began to show his impatience.

'Never mind old Lindauer,' he complained. 'You've come to talk to me.'

'That's right—so I have,' she smiled. 'Well—what's it all about? You said you're in trouble.'

'Yes, I am, but that can wait for a moment. Do you remember the days when we first met?'

'Of course. It's nearly three years ago. What about them?'

'I was new to the district and very lonely until your mother took me under her wing. And your father was most helpful when he offered good farming advice. You introduced me to your circle of friends and we went out together—remember?'

'What makes you imagine I've forgotten?' She suspected he was making an effort to stir old memories, but they left her cold.

'Anna seemed to be so much younger than you.'

'But she grew up—didn't she? Very rapidly, in fact.'

'Yes, she did, physically if not mentally. She's still little more than a child who demands the earth.'

'Ah—so you know her a little better now.' A wave of impatience swept her. 'Well—what's all this about? You said something about being in trouble.'

A worried frown crossed his face as an almost desperate look crept into his eyes. 'I'll be honest—I can't cope with Anna's extravagant ideas. She's determined to have a hundred or more alterations made to the house before I've done the important things first. I must replace the woolshed which is almost falling down. The yards need renewing—I must have another haybarn—and there's fencing to be done. Do you know what a mile of fencing costs these days? When I told Anna she laughed and wouldn't believe me. She could only gabble on about new carpets throughout the entire house. Wall-to-wall, of course.'

Julie felt a sudden rush of sympathy for him. 'Poor Ross—I can see your problem.'

He leaned forward and spoke earnestly. 'When I took over that farm it was a derelict run-down property. I'm gradually bringing it up to standard, but Anna's so demanding—I—I just can't see how I can handle it all.'

He attacked his food almost angrily for several minutes before he said, 'Of course there'll be stock to buy. You know the animal circle. In January I'll need at least five hundred replacement breeding ewes, five new rams and a new bull. Ten thousand dollars won't cover it.'

Julie sighed. She knew her sister's demanding ways only too well. What Anna desired she usually got for the simple reason she never let up until it was within her grasp. But why should Ross come to her about it? What he expected her to do was more than she could understand.

She said, 'I'm afraid Anna's still a small child who wants everything at once. She doesn't realise that things are appreciated more if they come gradually—that it's better to journey than to arrive.'

'If Anna loved me she'd try to understand the situation,' Ross growled. 'But oh no—she says that if I love her I'll do all the things she wants done to make her happy. It's a sort of checkmate.'

Julie looked at him searchingly. 'And—do you?'

'Do I love her? I don't know. I'm beginning to wonder about it. All this hassle has opened my eyes sufficiently to see her in a new light. It's caused my feelings to change and I'm afraid I've made a ghastly mistake.'

She stared down at her plate. 'Really? In what way?'

'I think I've put the ring on the finger of the wrong girl.'

Ted's words jumped into her mind. *Perhaps he'll admit he's backed the wrong filly.* It was so appropriate she wanted to laugh.

His voice became tense. 'Do you understand what I'm trying to tell you, Julie? I'm deadly serious about this.'

'I understand you're engaged to Anna and that you're allowing her to twist you into knots,' she retorted with some heat. 'As for what you're trying to tell me—I was never very bright at working out hints, innuendos and half statements. So you tell me—what, exactly, are you trying to say, Ross?'

He looked at her in silence for several moments, then, taking a deep breath, he lowered his voice which had suddenly become husky. 'I'd like to turn back the clock so that we could be as we were before—before all this happened. Don't you see? I want us to get together again.'

A flush of annoyance spread across her face. 'You dare to suggest this to me while you're engaged to my sister?'

'Believe me—it's an engagement that's nearly over. It'll have been one of the shortest on record in the district.'

She looked at him curiously. 'What makes you so sure I'd be any different from Anna?'

'Because I know you've got your feet on the ground while she's up in the air. Hell—I don't know what got into me.'

Julie found difficulty in knowing what to say him, especially as his situation was the result of her scheming younger sister's avid desire to have what she wanted. Ross had been taken in by her wiles, and she herself felt sorry for him. But she also recalled her own situation—the waiting and the longing for him to ask her to marry him. Nor was the shock of his engagement to Anna something she was likely to forget.

She said, 'You say you want us to be as we were before you and Anna became engaged. Does that mean we'll just continue to go out as good friends and nothing more?'

'Yes—for a while in the beginning. Later we'll become engaged.' He reached across the table to take both her hands, and, holding them in a firm grip he looked at her earnestly. 'I know you love me, Julie, so there's no need for you to deny it. If you didn't it was mighty strange that you should've rushed out of the house the moment Anna and I became engaged. No doubt it made you hopping mad, but your love for me will not be dead. It's still there——'

The anger that arose almost choked her. She snatched her hands away. 'Correction. I *thought* I loved you. I know, now, that I *didn't*. Please get that clear in your mind.'

'But you *could*—and you *would*,' he persisted.

'*Never*——' she declared vehemently on a slightly higher note. Then, suddenly embarrassed, she realised her voice had become raised, and the fear that others might be listening to their discussion caused her to glance at the nearby tables. The restaurant was now almost full and there was a general hum of conversation, but nobody appeared to be taking the slightest notice of them—except one person. Across the room she met the interested gaze of Adam Malvern.

He was sitting at a table with Elaine who looked striking in a flamboyant dress of bright golden yellow, her black hair swept up and caught in a sophisticated French roll at the back of her head.

Julie watched as he murmured a word then stood up and came towards their table. Her heart began to beat a little faster at the sight of his masculine virility and handsome face, although she recognised the trace of a scowl and the tightening of his jaw.

Pausing at their table he leaned forward to speak quietly, yet his words were clipped. 'Are you all right, Julie?'

She controlled her surprise. 'Yes—thank you, Adam. Why should you think I'm not all right?'

'Because I've been watching the play of expressions on your face from across the room, and they appeared to be anything but happy. In fact you seemed to be upset. I noticed your companion pawing your hands, and I saw you snatch them away. If he's being pest——'

Ross half rose to his feet. 'Now just you wait a minute, Buddy,' he began aggressively, but the quick pressure of Julie's hand on his arm made him pause.

Her light laugh was reassuring and hid the sudden glow that rose within her. Adam was concerned for her. She said, 'Oh no, he's not being a pest, but—but thank you, Adam.' She then introduced the two men.

Ross nodded offhandedly but did not bother to shake hands. Instead he sat and scowled.

Julie was infuriated by his rude attitude. She found herself searching for words to explain the fact that they were dining together. 'Ross is engaged to my sister so—so he'll soon be my—my brother-in-law,' she floundered. 'There was just a—a small matter he wished to discuss.'

'I see. One that makes it necessary for him to hold your hands?' His voice became heavy with sarcasm as he eyed Ross belligerently before turning to Julie. 'You're sure you're okay?'

'Of course I am. Thank you again, Adam.' She smiled at him. The inner glow was still there, making her grey eyes shine like twin pools and sending a radiance to her face. 'Perhaps you'd better go back to Elaine,' she suggested tactfully. 'She's looking very attractive this evening.'

'Yes. I'm making amends for having let her down when Fay had her pups.' His eyes softened unexpectedly as they rested upon her. 'Elaine isn't the only attractive person in this room—just in case you don't know.' The next instant he'd left them.

'Who the hell is he?' Ross snarled.

But Julie hardly heard him as she watched Adam make his way between the tables. He'd told her she looked attractive and she found difficulty in believing her own ears.

'Julie—you're not listening to me,' Ross snapped. 'Who is that fellow? Does he mean anything to you?'

'Oh—he's Adam Malvern,' she explained as she tried to disguise her satisfaction. 'Ted Lewis trains for him. You already know I'm staying with Ted and Molly.'

Enlightenment dawned upon him. 'He's the fellow your father spoke about the night Anna and I became engaged. I seem to recall your father hadn't a good word to say for him. What's he got against him?'

'Only the fact that he gave Ted a job after Father had sent him down the road.'

'If your father dislikes him I'm surprised to find you associating with him.'

'I can associate with whom I please—and it's certainly no business of yours——'

'Okay—okay—there's no need to get mad about it, but I'll say this—he sure brought the light to your eyes. A few words from him and you were all aglow. However, he appears to have an attachment by the look of that smart-looking dame with him.' Ross brushed the subject of Adam aside and returned to his former topic. 'Now then, let's talk about us——'

Julie interrupted him. 'Ross—I'm afraid you're moving along too quickly. When we spoke on the phone you said you're in trouble and that I'm the only one who can help you. All I can do is offer advice. You must tell Anna your exact financial position and she must be made to understand how much can be spent on alterations or—or whatever. It should be simple.'

'Don't you think I've tried that already?' He cut into his steak as though it offended him.

'She might think differently when you suggest breaking off the engagement because you fear the marriage isn't going to work. It'll be ruined by the constant load of debts. And if you imagine Anna will ever reach the stage of being satisfied, you're very much mistaken.'

He reached across the table to take her hands again. 'You really think I'd be wise to get out of this engagement situation?'

She longed to snatch her hands away again but she withdrew them gently. It was possible that Adam's eyes were still upon them and she had no wish to see him come striding across the room for the second time. Forcing herself to smile at Ross she said, 'The engagement situation is entirely due to your own actions. You'll have to get out of it in the best way you can.'

'Yes, I suppose you're right. And then—when that's all over—what about us?' His voice vibrated with eagerness.

She shook her head. 'Us? No, Ross, I'm afraid you'd be wasting your time. It's too late for there to be anything between us.'

'Nonsense. It's never too late. You loved me——'

Her patience was at a low ebb but she kept herself under control. 'Can't you understand? You've spoken about my love for *you*—but not one word have I heard concerning your love for *me*.'

'But you know it's there—deep down.'

'I don't know anything of the sort.' She laid her knife and fork on the plate and sat back, suddenly seeing him in a new light. 'You demand, but you don't give, Ross. You're exactly like Anna and that's probably why you both clicked so well. You're birds of a feather.' She paused to take a long breath. 'But as far as I'm concerned you can jolly well go and jump in the deepest part of the Gorge.'

His face became mutinous. 'You don't mean that.'

'I mean every word of it. Also, in future I'd be grateful if you'd sort out your own problems with Anna. Please don't come running to me with them because I'm not even remotely interested.'

His mouth took on a stubborn line. 'I'll definitely sort out the problem with Anna, but you needn't imagine you've seen the last of me. I'll be back—and we'll be together. You'll see.'

'I've told you—you'll be wasting your time.' She longed to get up and leave him there and then, but Adam's presence in the restaurant forced her to remain seated. It would amuse him to see her rush away from the table in obvious anger, therefore she sat and waited until Ross had finished his coffee.

It was a relief when they finally left the table, and as the account was being paid she glanced to where Adam and Elaine sat. He nodded briefly, while Elaine stared at Ross with unconcealed interest, a faint smile hovering about her lips.

Outside the restaurant Julie took rapid steps towards her Fiat, but Ross's firm hand on her arm held her back. 'What's the hurry?' he demanded. Then, in more pleading tones, 'Don't go home yet. Let's go for a drive. It's ages since you've been in the Rover.'

'No thank you, Ross, I'd prefer to go home.'

'Don't be silly—it can't do any harm.'

'Can't it? You're the one who's being idiotic if you think I'm getting into that Rover with you.'

'Okay—okay—but you'll at least kiss me good night.' His hand, still grasping her arm, twisted her round to face him.

She struggled but had little chance against his strength, nor at that moment, was there anybody nearby in the quiet street. '*How dare you——?* Kindly keep your hands off me,' she gasped.

He laughed. 'That's not what you used to say,' he reminded her as his lips descended upon her own.

The kiss was much more passionate than his previous

caresses, yet it roused no answering response in her. At last, as it ended, she looked up into his face and said, 'You said you want us to be together again. Is that something you really meant?'

'Yes—yes, it is. You *know* I want us to be together again.'

She took a deep breath then hissed at him, 'Then why are you doing your best to make me hate you?'

He released her abruptly. 'I'm sorry—I didn't realise. If I remember correctly you used to like my kisses.'

'But that was before you became engaged to my sister. Those times have gone, Ross. They're like water under the bridge.'

'I promise you those times will come again.' His voice gritted with determination.

'They'll never return for me, Ross—and I'll thank you to remember I don't want to see you again in this manner.' She got into the Fiat and slammed the car door. It felt safe there.

The window had been wound up but he shouted at her through it. 'And I'll thank *you* to remember that sooner or later you and I'll be married—so just get *that* stuck into your head——'

She wound the window down and again hissed at him, *'Go to hell.'*

The trusty little motor purred at the turn of the ignition key. She pressed the accelerator and it roared to life. A touch of the light switch flooded the road in front of the restaurant with beams, and there, standing on the footpath, was Adam Malvern. Even in the glow of the headlights she could see the sardonic expression on his face.

How long had he been there? she wondered. Had he observed Ross kissing her? Nor could he have possibly missed Ross's last shouted remark. No doubt it would amuse him. Miss Forsyth—dining with her sister's fiancé—blatantly kissing her sister's fiancé in the street. Miss Forsyth—smiling and agreeing while the aforesaid

fiancé promised to ditch the poor little sister and marry
her instead. How very typical of this girl who told lies,
he'd think.

CHAPTER SEVEN

ALTHOUGH the hour wasn't late the house was in darkness when Julie reached home. Even Tim's light had been put out because the early morning routine of saddling and brushing-up the horses meant long tiring days which called for sleep. She tiptoed inside, fearing to disturb Ted and Molly, and had just crept into her room when Molly, a warm blue wrap hugging her ample figure, came in and closed the door.

'Your father rang this evening,' she said. 'He's beginning to agitate for you to go home.'

Julie was startled. 'Oh? Did he have any special reason?'

'It seems that Anna isn't helping your mother as much as she could, therefore he demands your return. I pointed out that as Anna intends to get married she'd better learn to take over a household. He tossed that suggestion aside by saying that while he didn't mind you coming to stay with us for a few days, this was becoming ridiculous. I told him that as far as I'm concerned you can stay here forever.'

Julie gave her a hug. 'Bless you, Molly. I'll ring him in the morning, but—honestly—I don't know what to say to him. Even if I wanted to go home it—it'd be awkward.'

Molly looked at her curiously. 'Why should it be awkward? I don't want to pry—but are you saying something happened with your neighbour tonight?'

Julie sighed. 'I suppose you could say I've been given another chance with him, if I want it—which I don't.' She gave Molly an account of Ross's reason for wishing to talk to her. 'Do you see what I mean?' she asked pathetically. 'The moment I go home there's sure to be

114

trouble with Anna over Ross, although believe me, she's more than welcome to him.'

Molly's eyes were thoughtful. 'Yes—I can see what you mean, but there's no need for you to go home. You can stay here for as long as you wish.'

'Thank you, Molly. Perhaps I could make another dress for you—and then I could tell Father I'm too busy sewing to come home.'

'Tell him anything you please, but he has no right to bully you. After all, you've turned twenty-one.'

When Julie rang her father next morning his brusque tones made it clear he was displeased with her. 'It's time you came home,' he snapped. 'You can't expect me to continue paying you an allowance to help your mother when you're not here to do so.'

'Of course not, Father,' she agreed smoothly. 'It wouldn't be fair. Actually I'm spending so litle money here I can live on my savings for quite a long time.'

'Savings?' He snorted with derision. 'What sort of savings have you got? Next to nothing, I'll be bound.'

'Have you forgotten the money Gran left Anna and me? My share's in the bank on an interest-bearing deposit. If necessary I'd use it to help see me through until I come home.'

'You'd be a fool to break into it,' he snapped. 'You'd better speak to your mother. Perhaps she can talk some sense into you.'

When Claire Forsyth's voice came on the line she sounded worried. 'Is that you, Julie dear? Don't you want to come home?'

'Not at present, Mother. I have some sewing to do for Molly. I'm so thankful you made me take that course. I could never have made such a satisfactory job of the dresses I've made without it. I suppose Anna's busy sewing too—for her trousseau, I mean.'

'Anna——? Sewing——? You've got to be joking. She's waiting for you to come home and do it for her.'

'How is she?'

'She's all right, I suppose, although not as happy as an engaged girl should be. I can't understand what makes her so sulky when Ross comes here. There's something wrong, but I'm unable to put my finger on it. Actually, I'm quite worried about it.'

Julie took a deep breath. 'Mother—I don't want to interfere in Anna's affairs, but there's something I must tell you. I spoke to Ross last evening. He's not very happy, either, but I *can* understand why. Personally I think you'd be wise to have a quiet word in Anna's ear.'

'What on earth are you talking about, dear?'

'Well—she appears to be pushing him to spend more than he can afford. It's getting him down. If she's not very careful she'll find him opting out of the engagement. He'll run for it before it's too late for him to do so.'

Claire became exasperated. '*Opting* out? *Run* for it? I'm afraid I don't understand you, dear.'

'I'm talking about a broken engagement, Mother—due to the fact that she's a luxury too expensive for him to maintain. If I were you I'd look into the matter of what's upsetting Ross, rather than what's upsetting Anna.'

'I'll certainly do that—but how do you know about these things? You haven't been home to see them together.'

'I just—happen to know.'

'You said you were speaking to Ross?'

'I saw him in Woodville, but that's not important. The point is that unless Anna brings her sights down to the level of Ross's pocket there'll be no wedding.'

'You seem to know a great deal about it,' Claire said sharply.

'I know enough to tell you it's important for Anna to get the message. Goodbye, Mother—no—wait—I almost forgot to ask—how is Father managing with his new contact lenses?'

'Not very well, I'm afraid. He's still having difficulty in becoming used to them. They make him very cross.'

'Poor Father—why does he bother? Goodbye, Mother.'

As she replaced the receiver Julie turned to Molly. 'Do you think I said too much about Ross and Anna?' she asked anxiously.

'Not at all. I think it's better for your mother to be warned about the situation, but what can she do about it?' She giggled then said gleefully, 'At least I'm getting another new dress out of it. Tomorrow we'll take a drive to Palmy for more material—but today I must bake and get those cookie tins filled, otherwise I'd suggest we go at this very minute.'

But if they'd gone at that very minute they'd have missed an unexpected visit from Adam who walked into the kitchen as they were enjoying their morning coffee. Julie felt herself go hot at the mere sight of him, but Molly greeted him with a casual smile. 'Ted has gone to Woodville, but Tim's over at the stables,' she told him.

'How is the lad? Is he getting over his—er—posterior troubles? Have the pills taken effect?'

'Yes. He's started riding again, which relieves Julie.'

'Good. Well—I'll see Ted later. I've got Lucy in the car,' he surprised them by saying. 'I've realised she doesn't get out as much as she should.' The words were accompanied by a swift glance towards Julie.

'How can she get out unless somebody takes her?' Molly asked pointedly, tempering the words with a smile. She looked at Julie. 'See if you can persuade her to come in for a cup of coffee.'

Julie hastened out to the Peugeot where she found Lucy peering through the windows with interest. 'It's ages since I've been here,' the small woman admitted wistfully. 'The trees seem to have grown and the garden is so much brighter than I remember it.'

Julie opened the car door for her. 'Come and have

coffee,' she invited. 'After that I'll take you to see Gallant and Cloud.'

As they walked towards the house Lucy whispered, 'I was amazed when Adam asked me to come for a drive. He's been so much more thoughtful towards me lately. It seemed to begin after that day when you came to lunch.'

Julie smiled but said nothing.

Later, as Lucy sipped her coffee, she looked at Julie with that wistful expression that seemed to be part of her. 'I thought you'd have been back to see me before this,' she said. 'I've been hoping you'd come. Every morning I've thought—perhaps she'll come today.'

Julie sent an apologetic glance towards Adam. 'Well—really—I was waiting to be invited.'

Molly came to the rescue by hastening to put in an excuse. 'As it happens Julie's been very busy,' she explained. 'Her time has been completely taken up between riding the two horses and sewing for me. Come into the bedroom and I'll show you what she's made for me. She's very good at making dresses.' And taking Lucy's arm she led her from the kitchen.

There was a momentary silence after they had left the room, and for Julie there was tension simply because Adam stood looking at her. It made her nervous to find herself so conscious of his presence, and in an effort to control her fluttering emotions she became determined to let him speak first, otherwise she'd probably gabble inanely.

At last he said, 'Well—do you want to tell me about it?'

The question startled her. It was not one she'd expected. 'Tell you——? About what?' She turned to look at him, her eyes wide.

'About last night, of course.'

'I wasn't aware that it was any business of yours.'

'Ah—but I made it my business when I crossed the floor to see that you were okay.'

'I want you to know that I *did* appreciate it.'

'I came because you didn't appear to be over happy with that character whom you declared to be your sister's fiancé. Yet, later, I saw you kissing him quite blatantly in the street. You *did* say he's your sister's fiancé? I'm not mistaken about that?' His dark eyes held an accusing gleam as they rested upon her.

'No—you weren't mistaken.'

'When are they to be married—this fellow and your sister?'

'I don't know. Perhaps—never.' The last words slipped out before she realised she'd said them.

'Well—what's going on between you?'

She bristled angrily. 'Nothing's going on. If you've jumped to the conclusion that I'm having a clandestine affair with him, you're very much mistaken.'

'Then why did he come to see you? I was here when he phoned and arranged to meet you for dinner—remember?'

'There was something he wished to discuss. Do I have to remind you that it's not your business?'

'And what about your sister? Is it not her business that you're getting in a quick cuddle behind her back?'

'A quick cuddle behind her back?' She laughed suddenly. 'My oath—you don't know how funny that is. I suppose it's useless trying to explain that it was forced upon me. Anyhow—why should I bother? You've got your mind made up concerning the situation so I dare say that's that.' The fact that he thought so badly of her was like a knife wound she could do nothing to ease; and as for the frustration, it almost made her scream.

Mercifully, further discussion was curtailed as Molly and Lucy returned to the kitchen. Lucy looked at Julie with a new respect she made no effort to disguise. 'You're a very clever girl, dear. Molly's been most fortunate to have had you here. She put the dresses on to let me see how beautifully they fit her.'

Adam gave an amused laugh. 'Such praise will go to her head.'

Lucy turned upon him with a hint of irritation. 'It's all very well for you to laugh, Adam. You're one of the people who can just step into clothes, but I find trouble finding dresses to fit me. I'm so small the shop assistants usually send me to the teenage department, and then the styles are too young for me. I can tell you it's most frustrating when one has difficulty in buying clothes.'

'Let me make something for you,' Julie offered, the words being out before she'd given them a second thought.

Lucy's eyes shone with gratitude. 'Would you really make a dress for me?'

'Of course. Why not?'

Molly said, 'We're going to Palmy tomorrow for more materials and patterns. Would you like to come with us?'

'We'll be going in my Fiat,' Julie added, 'so if you don't mind driving in a small car——'

Lucy smiled happily. 'I'd love to come with you. I couldn't care less about the size of the car. It's ages since I've been over to Palmerston North.'

'There's no need to crush into the little Fiat,' Adam told them unexpectedly. 'I've a few matters to see to over there, so we'll all go in the Peugeot. I'll leave you in Broadway, then meet you for lunch at one o'clock.' His tone indicated that the matter was settled, nor did he bother to ask if the arrangements suited them.

'Thank you, Adam, that'll be lovely.' Lucy sounded gratified, then she appealed to Julie. 'Would I be allowed more than one piece of material?'

Julie laughed. 'Of course. Three or four, if you like. I'll soon make them up.'

'Oh—my dear—that'll be wonderful,' Lucy sighed, then added apologetically, 'I suppose I sound like a small child asking for a favour, but I do have trouble in getting a new dress.'

'Julie will need to give you several fittings for each dress,' Molly reminded her. 'How will you arrange it?'

Lucy hesitated. 'I—well—that's something I've been thinking about,' she admitted as she looked at Julie. 'When you've finished what you have to do for Molly would it be possible for you to come and stay with us at Malvern?'

Adam gave a short laugh that held little or no amusement. 'I wondered how long it would take for you to get round to asking her.'

His words gave Julie a slight shock. 'Does that mean you'd rather Lucy did not ask me to stay at Malvern? There's no need, you know. I can drive there and give her fittings without any trouble at all.'

Lucy began to protest. 'Oh no—I want you to come and stay with us. Please do—otherwise I'll be so disappointed——'

Adam shrugged. 'You see? She wants you to come, so you'd better do so. Obviously she's got her heart set on it.'

'But *you* don't want me to come,' Julie accused coldly.'

'I didn't say so.'

'You don't have to. It's written all over your face.'

Lucy stared from Adam to Julie then echoed her dismay. 'What's all this? Are you two having a quarrel? Is there antagonism between you?'

Julie turned to her. 'You might as well know the truth, Lucy. Adam doesn't like me very much. He's got me well and truly tabulated in his mind as being a deceitful liar. When we first met I didn't tell him my full name. I told him it was Julie Sterling, whereas it's Juliet Sterling Forsyth, and he's been looking for tricky, sneaky characteristics about me ever since. However, he's welcome to his opinion. It doesn't matter to me in the least,' she added, conscious of the deep hurt within her breast.

To Julie's surprise Lucy laughed. 'Is that all? Don't let it worry you, my dear. If you failed to tell him your full name you probably had a reason for doing so—and that reason's good enough for me. I flatter myself I can judge people.'

Julie breathed a sigh of relief. 'Thank you, Lucy.' she said quietly. 'It's nice to be trusted—for a change.' She flicked a brief glance towards Adam.

His mouth gave a wry twist. 'I'm sure it is.' Then he brushed the subject aside by turning to Molly. 'We'll pick you up at nine-thirty tomorrow morning. Will that be suitable?'

'Thank you—we'll be ready,' Molly promised.

Next morning they were ready before the appointed time. Lunch for Ted and Tim had been prepared and left waiting for when they came in, and Molly had also made a large stew of steak and several vegetables which would be heated and served at their evening meal.

Julie's nerves were on edge. She kept telling herself not to be an idiot, that this was just an ordinary shopping trip to Palmy, but she was unable to convince herself. How could a journey to any place with Adam be ordinary?'

At nine-thirty the clock in the front room had barely stopped chiming the half-hour when the green Peugeot pulled up near the back door. Lucy, sitting in the front seat, did her best to appear nonchalant, but her slightly flushed cheeks betrayed her underlying excitement and the fact that this was an unusual event for her.

She chatted brightly as they drove along the road, and when they were heading towards the Gorge she pointed to a large clump of trees on a hillside. 'There's a small cemetery beneath those elms and oaks,' she told Julie. 'Gottfried Lindauer is buried there. When you're staying with us would you mind driving me in your Fiat to see his grave?'

'I'm sure Julie has no desire to traipse round cemeteries,' Adam cut in a little harshly.

Surprised by his tone Julie met his eyes in the rear vision mirror. Their enigmatic expression puzzled her. Did he fear she'd become too friendly with Lucy—and was this something he wished to avoid? Forcing a smile she said, 'On the contrary I'd be interested to see the famous Lindauer's grave. Yes, Lucy—we'll certainly take a drive to see it.'

Lucy chatted on. 'When that restaurant was built and named the Lindauer there were mixed feelings in Woodville. Some people said it was an insult to the great artist, while others declared it would help keep his name alive. I believe the latter to be true. I'm sure many young people who have never heard of him have had his name brought to their attention just by having a meal in the restaurant. And there's a wine named after him——'

'All this free publicity is of little use to him now,' Adam commented drily. 'It's far too late. He's asleep under the oaks.'

He fell silent as he gave his attention to the road twisting through the Gorge. On their left the sheer height of growth-covered hillside rose up from the tarseal, while on their right the Manawatu river rushed with desperate urgency to find its way out of the narrow passage between the ravine walls.

Across the Gorge on a level with the road lay the railway line where diesel engines drew their string of carriages or trucks in and out of tunnels, their lowered speed indicating great respect for the line. Above it rose more bush-covered hills, richly clothed in a variety of greens too numerous to count.

The road became easier after leaving the Gorge. A long bridge took them across the river, and after passing commercial orchards and vegetable gardens they reached Palmerston North within a short time.

On more than one occasion during the drive towards the city Julie's eyes met Adam's in the rear-vision mirror. Their unsmiling stare made her wonder if he was annoyed with her, perhaps because she'd promised to drive Lucy to the small hillside cemetery. Or was it because of the possibility of her coming to stay with them? Perhaps it would be better if she didn't stay at Malvern.

She knew that Lucy couldn't possibly read her thoughts, yet it was strange that the small woman should choose that moment to turn round and say, 'I hope you've definitely made up your mind to come and stay with us. It'll be much easier if you do—and I'll be so disappointed if you don't.'

Adam's eyes met her own in the mirror again. They held a cold glint, yet his raised brows asked the unspoken question.

She stared back at him, almost defiantly. 'Yes, Lucy—I'll come,' she promised. 'As you say, it'll be easier for the fittings. Fortunately Ted won't need me any longer because Tim is now able to ride again.'

Adam made no comment. Ten minutes later he parked the car in Broadway near the cafe where they intended to have lunch, and which was within easy reach of several shops with good selections of dress fabrics. He gave the car key to Molly, pointing out that it would enable them to leave parcels in the vehicle, or give Lucy the opportunity to sit and rest in it if she felt tired. Then, with Molly promising to feed the parking meter, he left them, striding away to disappear among the people crowding the sheltered pavement.

The shopping spree for materials and patterns was completed by the time they were due to meet Adam for lunch. Molly made her choice among the piles of fabrics, and then care was taken over the purchases to be made for Lucy.

Only one small incident marred the day for Julie, and this occurred while they were having lunch. Adam had returned and had ushered them into the cafe where they were enjoying tea and sandwiches when one of her cousins paused beside the table.

'Hi—Julie——' she exclaimed brightly. 'What's going on between you and Anna and that guy next door? We all thought *you* were the one supposed to be getting engaged to him—and now we're told it's Anna. What's wrong with him? Couldn't he make up his mind?'

Julie was taken aback by the unexpected interrogation. 'That seems to be the situation,' she admitted, forcing herself to laugh in an effort to make light of it. At the same time she was conscious of the flush stealing up from her neck to her face, and she was also aware that Adam watched her through slightly narrowed lids. It was a relief when another girl came to drag her cousin away, warning her that she'd be late for work.

'*Cousins,*' Molly exclaimed crossly. 'You can't beat relatives for having their say on matters that don't concern them. Don't let it spoil your day,' she advised Julie in her motherly way.

Julie forced another light laugh. 'Oh no—they may think as they please.' She sent a level glance towards Adam. 'And that applies to other people as well.'

They left the city a short time later and were home by mid-afternoon. Adam assisted them with their parcels, and as Julie got out of the car Lucy turned to lay a hand on her arm. 'Please come as soon as you can,' she pleaded.

'I'll be there as soon as I've finished Molly's next dress,' she promised.

However, it was a week before she got there because, on opening her parcels, Molly admitted she'd bought two dress lengths instead of one. 'The opportunity was too good to miss,' she declared.

But at last the day came when Julie drove her red Fiat along the country road to Malvern, and as she drew near the homestead her emotions fluctuated between anticipation and nervous excitement. There was also a small amount of anxiety as she silently prayed that the dress making for Lucy would come up to the latter's expectations, and to give herself more confidence she patted Molly's sewing-machine which rested on the seat beside her. Molly had insisted upon her borrowing it because she suspected that the machine at Malvern would be old and perhaps not in the best of conditions.

It was late afternoon when she arrived. Lucy greeted her with delight, then led her into a downstairs bedroom which contained a table as well as the usual bedroom furniture. 'Would you be comfortable working in here?' she asked anxiously. 'I thought it would make a good sewing-room because of the table, the long mirror in the wardrobe, and there's a power point for the machine. You may sleep in an upstairs bedroom if you wish, or in this one if you'd prefer it. The downstairs bathroom is at the end of this passage. It's all quite close and handy.'

'This room will do nicely, thank you, especially with the afternoon sun streaming in through those nice large windows,' Julie assured her. Privately she decided that everyone else would be sleeping upstairs, and here she'd be in a small world of her own—but this thought was shattered by Lucy's next words.

'Elaine and I sleep upstairs but Adam's room is next to this one. He likes to be able to come and go without disturbing anyone,' she explained, 'particularly if he leaves early or comes in late at night and wants to take a shower.'

'Yes—I understand——'

'I hope you'll be able to use our old sewing-machine.' Lucy's tone was again anxious. 'It hasn't been put to work for ages.'

'Don't worry, I've brought Molly's Bernina because I'm used to it. I'll get settled in and start at once.'

It was a relief to have something to do, to find action of some sort that would help steer her thoughts away from Adam because the knowledge that he'd be in the next room was disturbing. She also knew that she must not torture herself by constantly listening for his step to come along the passage, or allow her imagination to tell her that he'd been with Elaine.

And with these decisions firmly fixed in her mind she carried her suitcase in, hung her clothes in the wardrobe and arranged her few cosmetics on the dressing-table. She then carried the sewing-machine in from the car. The table had to be pushed nearer the window so that the flex would reach the power point, and she was just taking the cover from the machine when Elaine walked into the room. She stood still and looked about her.

She said, 'Well—I really didn't believe Lucy when she said you'd be coming to sew for her. I told her that nobody makes dresses these days. It's so old hat—people just buy things.'

'Some people enjoy sewing,' Julie pointed out patiently.

'And just how well do *you* sew? Has Lucy seen any of your—er—creations, or is she running a risk by allowing you to hack into expensive materials?'

Julie refused to be needled. 'Lucy has already seen the dresses I've made for Molly.'

A shrill laugh escaped Elaine. 'Could she judge by that? I mean—poor Molly—all you have to do is run up the sides and throw a belt round her middle.'

Julie shrugged and said nothing. Why should she bother to explain the straight tailored lines of Molly's dresses, or the vertical stripes which helped to make her look slimmer?

But Elaine now had another question on her mind. Her sharp eyes had taken in the toiletries on the dressing-table, and the clothes hanging in the wardrobe. 'Surely you don't intend to sleep here?'

Julie looked at her with surprise. 'Why not——?'

'Because there are empty bedrooms upstairs. Guests are *never* put in this downstairs bedroom.'

'Lucy gave me the choice of an upstairs room, or, if I preferred to do so, I could remain in this one. I chose this one.'

Elaine spoke sharply. 'Lucy had no right to allow you to remain here. I run this house. Do you understand?'

'Not quite. I know you see to the meals and the housework, but I think of Lucy as being the hostess.'

'Then you can think again because those duties are also mine. I'll help you to carry your things upstairs.' She moved in a determined manner towards the wardrobe.

Julie took a firm stand by barring her way. 'I shall not move from this room. You can't make me go upstairs.'

Elaine's eyes narrowed. 'Why is it so important for you to remain downstairs? It wouldn't be because it puts you next to Adam, I suppose?' Her lip curled slightly. 'I can imagine you with a few ambitions in that direction.'

Julie flushed with anger. 'How dare you speak to me like this?'

A voice spoke from the doorway. 'Is something the matter? Do I detect—claws?' Adam stood regarding them both.

Julie turned an even deeper red, horrified by the thought that he might have heard Elaine's accusation.

But Elaine showed no sign of embarrassment. She gave a light laugh and said, '*Claws*——? Of course not. It's just that Julie imagines she can sleep in this room.'

He returned her look steadily. 'Is there some reason why she's unable to occupy it? Nobody uses it—and it's not haunted.'

Elaine smiled. 'Oh—she can *work* in it, but not *sleep* in it.'

'Why not?' he persisted.

'Well—because the rooms upstairs are more comfortable, and—and because she might disturb you.'

'You're saying she might—sleepwalk?' he asked casually.

Elaine sent him an angry glare. She tossed her head

slightly as a dull flush spread across her face, and although she opened her mouth to retort she remained silent.

Watching her, Julie sensed the anger and frustration bubbling beneath the surface, but was at a loss to define its real cause. Had Elaine found her way to Adam's room? And had he turned her round, pointed her in the direction of her own room and politely told her she was sleepwalking? Perhaps this was the true reason he was sleeping downstairs. Her heart lifted at the thought, but the next instant she was warning herself it was mere wishful thinking.

Elaine's irritation was still apparent as she said, 'Well—if she's determined to work and sleep here there's nothing I can do about it, but—considering that the rooms upstairs are so much nicer—her decision is quite ridiculous. Still—as it used to be a *maid's* room I suppose it'll be good enough for a *dressmaker*.' And flashing a baleful glare at Julie she left the room.

Adam moved to the table to examine the modern sewing-machine, then, glancing about the room with its single bed placed against the wall, he said, 'It's a nice sunny room to work in, but why do you want to sleep here as well? Elaine's right when she says the rooms upstairs are more comfortably furnished. You have a reason for wishing to stay so close to your work?'

'Yes. In that way I'll get it finished much more quickly. In the mornings I'll be able to make an early start on it, and in the evenings I can do a little before I go to bed.'

'Why all this slave-driving?'

'It'll hasten the day when I can leave your home and get out of your sight. I know you don't want me to be here. I've no illusions concerning your opinion of me, but I refuse to allow it to spoil my relationship with Lucy.'

'She'll be disappointed if you whisk through the job so that you can rush away within a short time. I understand she's landed you with four lengths of material. How long will it take you to make four dresses? Are they simple or complicated styles?'

'Not too plain, nor yet too dressy—and I'm afraid they'll take me at least a fortnight or longer. I'm not so expert that I'll be able to do them any quicker. I'm sorry if you think this is too long for my presence to be contaminating your house and the air you breathe——'

He swung round to face her. 'My oath—I could shake the living daylights out of you——'

But even as he took a step towards her, Lucy came into the room, her arms full of wrapped lengths of material, patterns, reels of sewing thread and zip fasteners. 'I haven't shown any of these pieces to Elaine,' she admitted nervously. 'I felt sure she'd find fault with every one of them.'

'So let's see them now,' Adam demanded angrily. 'Elaine has excellent taste, you know. She has a real flair for dress.'

'Yes—let's open them,' Julie agreed with forced brightness despite the fact that her heart was sinking. 'Let's have a *real* criticism from an expert. It'll be good to get it over and be done with it. You might as well know that I chose them all, and Molly gave her approval.' Her hands shook slightly as she unwrapped the parcels, then draped the materials over the table and the bed. She then placed the pattern pertaining to each length beside it.

He looked at them without speaking.

She went on to explain them individually. 'The skirt of this striped yellow, orange and brown cotton is cut on the cross so that it falls in soft folds. Lucy liked the high neckline.' She picked up the second pattern. 'This is a simple dress with several areas gathered, but for Lucy's slim form I'll probably put in a few extra gathers. The material with all these tiny squares of pink, purple and beige is known as a mosaic print.'

'It's very attractive,' he admitted grudgingly. 'I like this one too,' He fingered the third fabric.

'It's an easy-care jersey material. The colour is known as deep marine blue with contrasting confetti spots. The wide cut of the skirt is one that flatters small figures and it'll have long sleeves with contrasting collar and cuffs.' She turned to the last dress length. 'This floral material will also have long sleeves because it's for cooler days.'

'Well—what do you think?' Lucy asked anxiously. 'Do you approve of the materials and patterns?'

'Yes, I approve most heartily, but——' his eyes were cynical as they turned to Julie. 'Do you imagine you can complete all this in a mere fortnight? I'd say you'd have to be working for every hour of the day and night.'

She sent him a bleak look. 'Are you hinting you'd prefer that I do it in *less* time? If so you've only to say and I can at least try. Please don't hesitate to speak your mind——'

'What nonsense is this?' Lucy snapped, glaring from one to the other. 'You're *quarrelling* again——'

Adam ignored her. 'We'll talk about it later,' he said to Julie, his tone unexpectedly harsh. He then left the room abruptly.

Perplexed, Lucy shook her head. 'I don't know what gets into him. He never used to have these moods.'

Julie made an attempt to brush him from her mind. 'Never mind his moods. Tell me which dress you'd like to have made first and I'll cut it out this evening.'

Lucy brightened visibly. 'Oh—well—with the warmer days coming I'd like the mosaic print.'

'Right. Now let me take your measurements.'

She worked steadily, pausing only to eat the evening meal, and returning to the bedroom as soon as it was over. The pattern was studied, the material laid on the floor and the thin pieces of paper were placed in position. It was the easiest of the four dresses to be made, and for this she was grateful as it gave her the feel of Lucy's slight figure before working on the more detailed garments.

By the time she was ready for bed the dress had been cut out and neatly pinned together. Later she would tack it. Nor did she find concentration easy as thoughts of Adam kept intruding into her mind. She realised he'd scarcely looked at her during dinner, yet she felt sure he had something simmering at the back of his brain.

We'll talk about it later, he'd said. Talk about what? she wondered.

She recalled he'd made a similar statement when they'd stood beneath the portrait of Ana Rupene—but then it had been *see you later*. And somehow those words had led to the cave with the waterfall. She shook herself mentally, telling herself she was being ridiculous. There was no connection between what he'd said then and what he'd said during today's late afternoon. Yet, despite herself, her heart began to beat a little faster as anticipation fluttered in and out of her senses, building itself into something she knew she must control.

At last she folded the sewing neatly, placing the pieces in a pile on the table and scanning the floor for fallen pins. A short period of reading in bed then helped to clear her mind of its darting thoughts, and she was about to switch off the light when a tap sounded on the door.

'Come in——' she called, fully expecting Lucy or Elaine.

But it was neither. The door opened and Adam came in. He closed it quietly and crossed the room to sit on the side of the bed.

CHAPTER EIGHT

JULIE's heart thumped at the sight of him. She sat bolt upright, clutching the bedclothes and dragging them up beneath her chin. Her mouth went dry and her voice sounded husky as she said, 'What do you want? I thought it was Lucy or—or Elaine.'

'The first thing you can do is to simmer down and relax. You're not going to be raped. I said we'd talk later, didn't I?'

'What is there to talk about?' Her grey eyes were still wide, while behind her head the reading-lamp attached to the back of the bed threw a nimbus of light through her honey-gold hair.

He looked at it and said, 'You've got a halo which makes you appear almost angelic. It belies the little spitfire hiding deep down under your skin.'

'Spitfire? Surely that's an exaggeration. It's just that I refuse to lie down under insults, especially when they're unjust. Was it my character you've come to discuss?'

'No. It's Lucy. I suppose you can see she's taken a great fancy to you,' he declared bluntly.

'That, also, is an exaggeration—although I'll admit I've taken rather a fancy to her. She's such an inoffensive, sweet little person, I feel I want to do things for her.'

'Then why rush at full speed over the sewing of these dresses? Why not give her the pleasure of your company for as long as you can? Or is it really necessary for you to return home?'

'No—I can't go home yet,' she said with more force than she intended, then immediately regretted the words.

'Can't go home? Why not?' He regarded her intently.

'You—you wouldn't understand. Nor do I wish to discuss it.'

'Have you quarrelled with your parents? Is it that crusty old man of yours? I've heard he's got a short temper.'

'No—I have *not* had a row with my parents. I know Father can be difficult, but I'll thank you to remember he *is* my father.'

'Okay—okay—at least you're loyal to him. So if it's not your parents it must be your sister. Ah—I see it all! It's your sister and her fiancé—the man with whom you dined at the Lindauer. The trouble's there—isn't it?'

'Don't you mean the man you saw me kissing in the street?' Her voice became scathing. 'I know that's what you're *really* thinking.'

'I'll admit the scene is rather vivid in my mind. Want to tell me about it? I know you refused to tell me when I asked you about it next morning, but perhaps you've changed your mind.'

'No—I have not—thank you.'

'Very well, it really doesn't matter. Your cousin in the café in Palmerston gave a fairly clear gimpse of the picture. From what she said I've guessed he pursued you both, but finally decided upon marrying your sister.'

'And in my underhand way I'm trying to lure him away from her. Is that what you think?' Again her tone was scathing.

'Why don't you tell me the truth of the matter?'

'There's no need. Your mind's already made up.'

'You know absolutely nothing of what's in my mind—and that's something else I want to talk about. I'd be grateful if you'd stop uttering remarks that make Lucy think I dislike you.'

'But it's a fact. She might as well know the truth.'

'It's not a fact—it's a long way from the truth.'

'No——? You *don't* think I'm a deceitful liar—that I'm *not* trying to steal my sister's fiancé—and that you *like* to have me in your home? My oath—you could've fooled me.' Her voice rose slightly while the sudden rush of tears to her eyes infuriated her. She turned away, blinking at them rapidly.

Perhaps it was the sight of the tears that moved him to compassion because even before they disappeared his arms were about her, holding her in a grip from which she made no attempt to struggle.

Hardly daring to believe that the feel of them was real she whispered, 'I hate knowing you think of me in that manner. I try to tell myself it doesn't matter—that I don't care——'

'But you do——?'

'Deep down it really hurts.' Her head rested against his shoulder and she felt his fingers beneath her chin, gently but firmly tilting her face upward.

'Perhaps this will convince you that I don't think of you like that,' he murmured against her lips. The kiss was long and tender as his arms tightened about her and his lips took possession of her soft mouth. At last he said, 'I'll admit I was mad when I knew you hadn't told me your full name. Nor was I amused when it was Elaine who came to light with the Forsyth part of it.'

She stirred uneasily in his arms. Even while holding her close to him he could think of Elaine, she noticed. 'Ah—yes——' she murmured. 'At this moment aren't you being somewhat unfaithful to Elaine? I mean— *speaking of deceit*——'

He chuckled. 'Poking the bone at me, are you? Let me assure you that Elaine's hopes of pinning me down faded a long time ago.'

'Oh? I thought she had a special claim on you.'

'No. It's her mother who has the claim on me. She was always very kind to my own mother, and now that she needs a fatherly eye kept on her property I feel I must do what I can for her.'

'Yet—Elaine must mean something to you,' she

persisted. 'You must've become—close—over the years.'

'What are you trying to say?'

She remained silent, unable to put her thoughts into words. She knew he was a man whose masculine virility had endowed him with the normal male sensual needs, and the natural hunger to make love to a woman who could match his own ardour—yet at the same time this kowledge rang a warning bell and told Julie she must keep a cool head.

'Well—come on—out with it,' he probed. 'Are you suggesting that Elaine and I are having an affair that isn't getting any place at all?'

'She must fit into your emotional life—somewhere——'

'Oh no, she doesn't. She's a damned good house-keeper, but apart from that she has no more claim on me than any other friend of long standing. Did you imagine there was a commitment between us?'

'To be honest—I did wonder about it.'

He didn't love Elaine, she realised with a sense of overwhelming relief. In fact she doubted that he was in love with any woman he knew—least of all herself.

During the time he'd been speaking of Elaine his arms had slid from her body, enabling her to snuggle down between the sheets. He then moved his own position to lie on the bed, the length of his body stretched beside her although the blankets were between them.

Rolling on his side to face her, his eyes raked her features until they rested upon her mouth. He kissed it again, lightly this time, then trailed his lips across her brow, her cheeks, her jawline and neck. 'Anything else you'd like to know?' he murmured against the softness of her throat.

His caresses were making her feel breathless. 'No,' she managed to say at last. 'It's just that I wouldn't like to—to hurt Elaine if she's somebody special to you—— '

He gave a short laugh. 'Thank you for the confidence in my fidelity.'

'I'm sorry—I didn't mean——'

'I know exactly what you meant. You're accusing me of two-timing Elaine. Well—you can get the idea right out of your head.' He drew a deep breath as though shaking the thought of Elaine from his mind. His hand slid beneath the bedclothes to gently massage the muscles of her back, and as his lips found hers once more she felt the fire leaping through her veins.

Suddenly he drew back and stared at her intently. 'Now then—I want to know the situation between you and your sister's fiancé.' His tone was abrupt, demanding an answer.

She was startled. 'There's nothing to know—there's no situation. There might've been once, but there certainly isn't now.'

'You're forgetting I witnessed that embrace in the street outside the Lindauer, therefore I'm sure there is. Do I have to wring it out of you?'

Resigned, she said, 'Very well—although I can't understand why you're even remotely interested. He's our neighbour as I've already told you, and he pursued us both—as you've already guessed. Eventually he preferred my sister to me. It's as simple as that.'

She fell silent, unable to lay before his eyes the scene of her own heartbreak. Nor could she admit how very much she'd longed to become engaged to Ross, nor tell of the shock of learning he'd asked Anna to marry him, and that this was the reason she'd fled to Molly and Ted.

But he dug for more details. 'You loved this man?'

'I thought I did. I know—now—that I didn't.'

'Okay—just a few more questions. Did he come to tell you he'd made a mistake about his engagement to your sister?'

'Well—yes—he seemed to be hinting in that direction.'

'I'd say hinting is the understatement of the year. Watching him from across the room I could see he was being very definite about whatever he had on his mind. As Ted so aptly put it—he'd backed the wrong filly.'

'Yes—I suppose so,' she admitted reluctantly as she became aware that Adam was being far too astute in his summing up of the whole situation.

'And you—what do you feel for him now?'

'Nothing at all.' She lifted her face as her arms went about his neck. 'Would I be lying here—with you—if I loved Ross Mitchell? I was never as close to him as this——'

A small sound escaped Adam as he swept the bedding from between them and crushed her against the male contours of his body. His hand brushed aside the flimsy shoulder straps of her nightdress, and as he buried his face in the cleavage between her swelling breasts her body cried out to him, filled with desire such as she'd never known.

But at the same time the alarm bells rang in her head, clanging the warning that this could be a man who would take her—and then leave her. They brought her to her senses and gave her enough strength to gasp, 'No Adam—*no*. Please stop——'

He looked at her in a dazed manner. 'I thought you felt as I do—I thought you wanted me as much as I need you——'

She stared at him aghast. 'I *want* you—you *need* me? There's a mighty big difference.' How could she tell him she wanted him because she loved him, and that he needed her merely to satisfy his own sexual desires. Nor did she intend to be used in this way.

'So—you're the lead-'em-on and then turn-'em-down type,' he rasped furiously, his face pale.

'You can think anything you like. Is this all you came in here for?' she demanded angrily. 'All this pretence of—of I'll talk to you later! Huh! And you dare to say *I'm* deceitful. All you want is to *use* me——' She began to weep quietly, the tears rolling unheeded down her cheeks.

'We seem to have misunderstood each other,' was all he said as he stood up and glared at her before striding from the room.

After he'd gone she lay awake for a long time, telling herself she hated him, but knowing perfectly well that she did not. She knew she still loved him, and even while she thought of him as one who would use her merely to satisfy his own sensuality, she found herself making excuses for him. He was a man—and men did these things.

Eventually she fell into a restless sleep that was plagued by a dream which carried her out on to a steep hillside. When she looked up the heights seemed to be out of sight, and when she looked down it was into a deep abyss. It was a relief to wake up, and it took several moments to realise she was in Adam's home.

Thoughts of the previous night's events swept into her mind, but instead of stirring her to anger they spun round the memory of his arms holding her close to him, his lips on her breast, the length of his body stretched beside her own. It was all such a new experience for her—something she would never forget.

She shook herself mentally, telling herself she was being a fool. Perhaps the episode was best forgotten. And with this decision firmly fixed in her mind she sprang out of bed, slipped into her wrap and ran along the passage to the bathroom. It had been used already that morning, she noticed, therefore, on reaching the kitchen for breakfast, she was not surprised when Lucy told her that Adam had left the house hours earlier.

'Didn't you hear him go?' Elaine asked. 'Sound is apt to carry in this house,' she added mockingly. 'For instance, I know he was in your room last night. Mine is just above it and I heard the murmur of your voices.'

Julie remained calm. 'I hope we didn't disturb you. Adam had something he wished to discuss with me.'

'Oh——? Such as——?' Elaine demanded sharply.

A vague smile crossed Julie's face. 'Oh—this and that,' she said evasively. 'The price of fish and whether rhubarb will be expensive this year——'

Lucy giggled, 'And why the sea is boiling hot and whether pigs have wings——'

'Sorry I asked,' Elaine snapped angrily.

'I'd been working on the mosaic material when he walked in,' Julie informed them casually. This was quite true. She *had* been working on that particular fabric, nor did she consider there was any need to tell them she was in bed when he arrived.

'It's almost ready to wear, I suppose?' Elaine's sneer was barely concealed.

'Not quite. It's cut out and the darts have been atended to. Is there an iron and an ironing-board I can use? I like to press the seams as I work.'

'Of course. They're in the laundry.' Lucy led her to a small room opposite the back door, then watched as Julie set up the ironing-board in the bedroom. 'Please don't hurry to much with these dresses,' she pleaded wistfully. 'I don't want you to leave before you really have to. There are so few people for me to talk to.'

'I won't rush them,' Julie promised. 'I'm not a professional dressmaker, and I always make mistakes when I try to do things too quickly. I loathe having to unpick machine stitching.'

'Good. Then you can take a nice long time over them,' Lucy said with undisguised satisfaction as she left Julie to get on with the job.

But despite the promise that the dresses would not be rushed Lucy found her own methods of extending operations. She insisted upon Julie taking breaks every morning and afternoon to walk round the grounds. Sometimes they went to admire the brilliance of the azalias blooming beneath the blossom-laden flowering cherry trees, and at other times to the orchard where the old pear trees stretched branches of massed white blooms against the blue of the sky. Fay and her pups were paid visits, and although Julie kept her eyes open for the sight of Adam's tall figure, she saw very little of him.

It's almost as though he's avoiding me, she thought miserably as she noticed that he came in late for meals and left almost before anyone else had finished.

Lucy also noticed his short-lived appearances. 'We hardly see you,' she complained.

'I've been busy,' he told her blandly and without apology. 'I've been checking the flock for Elaine's mother, to say nothing of keeping an eye on things at home. I've also been spending time at the stables. Gallant is doing three-quarter pacework on the plough during this week and next week.'

'That means you'll be racing him soon?' Julie asked. She was determined to make him stop ignoring her, and as he turned to face her his dark eyes seemed to bore into her mind with unspoken questions that caused her colour to rise.

'Yes, if he appears to be fit enough at the end of next week when the races will be here at Woodville.'

She wondered if Big Boy would be running but decided it would not be diplomatic to mention his name. It would be awkward enough when the day came, especially if he ran in the same race as Gallant and beat him again. If that happened she'd probably be wise to creep out of the house and completely disappear.

'The dressmaking progresses well?' Adam asked politely, the question being put more to Lucy than to Julie.

Lucy beamed. 'My mosaic pattern dress is now ready to wear and I'm delighted with it. Even Elaine says it looks nice and has been well finished off—you know—the underneath part.'

The dark brows shot up. 'Really? This must be praise indeed.'

'You'll be glad to know the second dress is well on the way,' Julie told him, 'so it won't be long——' She looked at him meaningly, the message being that she'd soon be out of his house.

He returned the stare coolly. 'If you've been working so hard you probably deserve a break. Weren't you going to drive Lucy to see Lindauer's grave?'

Elaine turned to Julie. 'You certainly deserve time off,' she said unexpectedly. 'Why don't you go this afternoon after Lucy's had her sleep and a cup of tea? It'll give your eyes a rest from so much close work.'

'Yes—she does need a rest. We'll go this afternoon,' Lucy decided, looking pleased about the prospect.

Julie found difficulty in disguising her surprise. It wasn't like Elaine to be considerate on her behalf and she couldn't help wondering about it. Did she want Lucy and herself out of the house for some reason? Did Adam intend to be home this afternoon? He was the one who'd suggested the outing, she realised. Well—it didn't matter what either of them had in mind, she'd take Lucy for the promised drive which at least would be a pleasant change.

It was late afternoon when they left. Lucy wore her new dress and they called in at the stables to show it to Molly. It was much admired and Lucy was told how smart she looked.

'How are the horses?' Julie asked. 'I miss that lovely Cloud.'

'Both fit and well,' Molly reported. 'Next week they'll have Gallant doing fast work after his three-quarter pacework—and you know what *that* means.'

'It means they intend to race him,' Lucy declared knowledgeably. Molly and Julie looked at each other but said nothing. Both knew the other was thinking about Big Boy, and then Julie's thoughts slid to her parents. Mother and Lucy would get on well together she felt sure, and then it only needed Father and Adam to meet and like each other. But after all—what difference would it make?

They left Molly and drove to Woodville where they turned on to the main highway, then headed towards the Gorge. The small hillside cemetery was soon reached, and after crossing the railway line they turned into the short rough metal drive that twisted uphill beneath cypress trees and evergreens with weeping foliage which seemed to emphasise the area as a place of mourning.

The graves lay on terraces which were sheltered from the strong westerly winds by a high grassy knoll which was studded by outcrops of limestone. The paths between the rows lay beneath the spreading boughs of oaks and elms in new leaf, and a wooden fingerpost nailed to the trunk of an oak pointed the way to Lindauer's grave.

Lucy led Julie up the slanting path towards it. The unusual headstone was appropriately formed in the shape of an artist's palette set in a low block of granite. Julie read the inscription aloud. 'In loving Memory of Gottfried Lindauer. Artist. Born in Pilsen, Bohemia, January 5th 1839. Died June 13th 1926. Rest in Peace.' She stared at the length of concrete, now weathered to a dull grey. 'It's so difficult to believe that there lie the bones of the fingers that painted portraits which are now famous,' she added quietly, her mind's eye seeing the face of Ana Rupene.

'Lindauer's small studio still stands in Woodville,' Lucy told her. 'In 1885 one of his paintings of a Maori girl, known as *Poi Girl*, was presented to the Prince of Wales who later became Edward the Seventh, so he really did make a mark in the art world.'

'Adam is fortunate to have so much of his work,' Julie said, her thoughts still on Ana Rupene. *See you later*, he'd declared Ana to be saying. And later he'd taken her to see the waterfall in the cave. She sighed as she recalled the feel of his arms, the pressure of his lips.

Lucy gave a sudden shiver. 'It's time we were going home. I hate cemeteries, but I wanted you to see his grave.'

Very little was said on the way back to Malvern because Julie and Lucy were both engrossed with their own thoughts, but as they approached the entrance Lucy's hand patted Julie's arm. 'Thank you dear, that was a pleasant outing. I wish I'd learnt to drive a car years ago.'

The house was strangely silent when they went inside. There was no sign of Elaine preparing the evening meal, but as they walked into the hall the sound of her laughter floated down from the upper landing.

Adam's voice reached them. 'I'd prefer you to keep this affair to yourself. Do you understand?'

'You mean it's to be our secret?'

'If you like to think of it in that way—at least until I do something definite about it.'

'Dear Adam—Mother will be so surprised. It'll be quite a shock for her.'

'Not only for your mother——' His deep tones held amusement.

Julie felt herself go cold as their words floated down the stairs. What did Adam mean by an affair that must be kept secret until he'd done something definite about it. Had he discovered himself to be in love with Elaine after all? Was there an engagement in the air—one he didn't wish to have made public before he'd put the ring on her finger?

Lucy it seemed, was also perturbed, her mouth tightening as she looked towards the upstairs landing. 'Are you there, Adam?' she called. 'We're home now——'

He came to the head of the stairs. 'Yes—I'm here. Elaine and I are having a private discussion. Did you want me for some reason?'

'No. I—I just wondered where you were. I'm sorry if I disturbed you—we won't interrupt.'

Elaine appeared from behind him and began to descend the stairs. 'Don't worry—we'll continue this discussion later,' she said as she threw a glance full of meaning towards Adam. She looked composed although slightly flushed, and there was a bright sparkle in her eyes which made her look more attractive than usual.

Julie thought she detected a hint of quiet triumph in the smile Elaine sent towards her, but the next instant she was trying to assure herself she'd imagined it. Determined to remain on friendly terms she said, 'Can I help you prepare the evening meal?'

Elaine's attitude became lofty. 'No thank you. I'm more than capable of doing it myself. One has to be in this house, you know. Did you find old Lindauer's grave?'

'Yes—it's such a peaceful place,' Julie said. 'Some of the dates are quite early. I couldn't help remembering a few lines of Gray's 'Elegy'.'

Elaine looked blank. 'Gray? Who is he? I've never heard of him. Someone you know, I suppose?' Her lip curled slightly.

Adam's brows shot up as he expressed his surprise. 'Are you saying you've never heard of Gray's 'Elegy' written in a country churchyard? It's an English classic.'

Elaine shrugged. 'Not even remotely have I heard of it.'

He looked at her in silence for several moments before turning to Julie. 'Which lines came to your mind?'

Julie sent a nervous glance towards Elaine, plagued by the suspicion that in some intangible way she was about to bring an avalanche of wrath upon her head. However, in answer to Adam's question she said, 'It's not really a churchyard, yet it's so appropriate in its fourth verse. Do you remember those lines?

Beneath those rugged elms, that yew-tree's shade,
Where heaves the turf in many a mouldering heap,

Each in his narrow cell for ever laid,
The rude forefathers of the hamlet sleep.

Elaine gave a brittle laugh. 'You think you're very
smart being able to gabble off a few lines of poetry.
Anyhow—I hate cemeteries. They depress me. I'm glad
I wasn't there with you. It was much nicer here with
Adam. He's so *vital*—so *alive*.' Her eyes glowed as she
gazed at him.

Julie turned to observe Adam's reaction to Elaine's
enthusiasm concerning himself, but she learnt nothing.
His face was a mask. Then, finding herself unable to
look at him she went to her bedroom and began to
study the pattern for Lucy's striped dress.

She didn't hear Adam follow her until he came into
the room.

'How long had you been standing at the foot of the
stairs before Lucy called to me?' he asked casually.

'Long enough,' she informed him vaguely.

'Long enough for what?' he snapped.

She sent him a direct stare. 'Long enough to learn
that you and Elaine have an intriguing secret between
you.'

'A secret? Is that all?' He watched her closely, his eyes
raking her face before lingering upon her lips.

Her heart contracted. 'Surely—it's enough. I presume
it's of an emotional nature.'

'You presume? Didn't you hear enough to tell you
what it was about? I don't recall our voices being
lowered.'

'We were there for only a few moments. We weren't
eavesdropping—as you suggest.' She fell silent, longing
to ask him the direct question, and after several
moments of hesitation she said, 'I suppose you and
Elaine will be announcing your engagement within a
short time.'

He gave a shout of laughter, then snatched her to
him, scattering the flimsy pieces of paper pattern to the

floor. 'Would it concern you if that happened to be the case?' he asked.

She stared up into his face, her eyes defiant. 'Why should it? I mean nothing to you, so what do my thoughts matter?'

'Would it surprise you to learn they definitely matter to me?'

'It certainly would—and it's hard to believe.'

She decided she must be dreaming. *He cared about her thoughts?* His words had lifted her spirits and she lowered her head lest he read the tell-tale message of love in her eyes. The roughness of his jacket against her cheek was definite evidence that he was holding her closely, and she tried to stamp the feel of it on her brain. Later it would be nice to remember——

Although she kept her eyes lowered she knew his fingers beneath her chin were raising her face, and that his lips were about to meet her own. The next moment she was clinging to him with her usual lack of control. The blood rushed through her veins, and while she knew she was only building up heartache for herself, she seemed powerless to resist the thrill of being close to him, the magnetism of his kiss that sent her senses reeling with wanton abandon.

At last Adam said, 'Does that convince you I'm not engaged to Elaine—that things are not as you suspect?'

She shook her head. 'Not really. Men are so changeable—so unpredictable. Besides—the alliance between you is supposed to be secret. It leaves you so free.'

He shook her angrily. 'Listen to me, you distrusting little devil, the secret between Elaine and myself concerns the man working on her mother's property. Elaine has been told he's doing a fiddle with the stock. The losses he reports are really being sold to a friend. Do you understand? I've asked her to say nothing about it until I've looked into the matter.'

'And—and that's the secret between you?'

'Nothing more—nothing less.'

Julie was so relieved she wanted to weep, but instead she leaned against him and began to giggle. However, it was mirth that lasted only a short time because Elaine spoke from the doorway.

'Am I interrupting something important?' she asked in icy tones.

Adam released Julie gently. 'Not really. Julie was in need of reassurance—that's all.'

'Nothing more?' Elaine's voice was still cold.

'Nothing more,' Adam said. 'Did you want me for something?'

'Lucy wants more firewood brought in. Perhaps you could lay Miss Forsyth aside for long enough to build up the fire.' Sarcasm dripped from each word.

CHAPTER NINE

LIFE at Malvern moved along smoothly for the next week although Elaine's attitude towards Julie was decidedly cool. Little was seen of Adam, and she presumed he was busy on the farm or at the stables. Nevertheless there were times when he appeared unexpectedly, and then her heart leapt as it sent the blood rushing to her face. This was disconcerting because she knew that even after she left this place the mere thought of him would bring a secret longing she'd be unable to control.

On one occasion he paused beside her as she sat in the sun busy with some handwork. 'Lucy's taken a new lease of life since you've been here,' he told her. 'What have you done to achieve this change in her?'

She threaded a needle, then chose her words carefully. 'I've done nothing except treat her as one who is very little older than myself—instead of one who is a useless geriatric.'

Adam frowned in sudden anger. 'Is that how you imagine I've treated her?'

Julie kept her eyes on her work. 'To be honest I suspect she's been treated as part of the furniture and taken for granted. Have you ever put your arms about her and given her a hug? Have you ever let her know you're grateful to her for stepping into the breach when your mother died?'

'If I did she'd think I'd gone mad.'

'Perhaps your failure to do so has made her feel you have very little affection for her.'

'My oath—you don't pull your punches.'

Julie bit her lip. 'I'm sorry—I had no right to make such a statement.' She knew the words had been prompted by her own inner frustration—her own longing to feel his arms about herself and to cope with it she concentrated more carefully on her work, picking up a single thread as she stitched an invisible hem.

The dressmaking continued to progress without undue haste, mainly because Lucy refused to allow Julie to work without interruption. She made sure they drove to the township for groceries and fruit, that they took walks in the garden which was becoming bright with spring flowers, and on two occasions she asked Julie to drive her to visit elderly friends whom she hadn't seen for years.

It was after one of these outings that Adam came into her room. 'I've a message for you from Molly,' he said. 'She rang this afternoon when you were out but, as Elaine was most unco-operative, I said I'd pass it on to make sure you got it. She said to tell you that Ross Mitchell called to see you late this afternoon.'

'Oh? What did he want?' She was conscious of a sinking sensation. She had no wish to see Ross.

'Adam's eyes were mocking. 'I don't know what he's got in mind, but I suppose it's easy to guess.'

'Is it——?' She kept her voice cool.

'He'll probably turn up sooner or later and then he'll be able to tell you himself. I'm sure it'll be interesting.'

'Are you saying Molly told him where to find me?'

'No. Actually it was Tim. When Molly refused to divulge your whereabouts he went stamping off to the stables to find somebody else, and of course he found Tim. Naturally, it was no trouble for Tim to say where you were and to tell him how to get here. Nor is it any use being mad with Tim because he wouldn't know who this man happens to be. Tim's boils have completely disappeared now——'

'I don't want to talk to Ross,' she cut in.

'You're sure? I've been wondering about it.'

'I've *told* you, haven't I? Why should you wonder about it?'

'Because—deep down—I think you're still interested in him. Also—I've got a feeling about him. I think he means business.'

Julie was thoughtful. She also feared that Ross meant business. In some vague way he'd changed from the Ross she used to know, the man who'd found difficulty in making up his mind. Now he seemed to know exactly what he wanted and was determined to get it. But whatever Adam imagined her own feelings to be they were certainly not directed towards Ross Mitchell. Still—perhaps it wouldn't hurt to be polite to Ross—if Adam happened to be watching.

During dinner the thought of Ross's arrival ruined her appetite to such an extent that Elaine noticed that she merely picked at her food. 'Is there something wrong with the steak?' she demanded.

'No—of course not. It's just that I'm not hungry.' Julie smiled to give assurance.

'She's on edge,' Adam teased. 'She's expecting a visitor.'

Lucy was interested but Julie refused to be drawn into any explanations, passing the suggestion off lightly.

When the meal was over Lucy and Elaine became engrossed in a television programme, but Julie felt too restless to settle to it. She watched it for a short time then walked outside to find the garden clearly defined by the light of the full moon. The snowball tree near the end of the veranda stood in ghostly splendour, its branches laden with globes of white flowers, while the perfume of the lilacs growing on the edge of the lawn caught her senses. Breathing in the heady fragrance she went towards them.

She had almost reached them when a mocking voice spoke from behind her. 'Waiting for him?' Adam had followed her across the lawn.

Startled, she swung to face him, the moonlight accentuating the pallor of her face and making his handsome features look gaunt. She drew a deep breath.

'Certainly not. It's just that I needed a little fresh air——'

'—and time to ponder—to make your decision,' he added.

She laughed. 'That's what you're determined to think.'

'If you'd like to know what I *really* think I'll soon tell you, although you mightn't like it. It means I'll have to be blunt.'

'I dare say I can take it.'

'Well—if you must know—I believe your decision has already been made. You'll take him back.'

She was astounded, and at the same time curious. 'What on earth makes you so sure about that?'

'Your kisses have been enough to tell me.'

She gaped up at his shadowed face. 'My—my kisses? I don't understand. How could they possibly tell you anything?' Her cheeks began to feel hot.

'Do you recall the short time we spent in the cave? I held you in my arms like this——' His arms went about her, holding her to him. 'And I kissed you. Remember?'

She lifted her face. 'How could I forget those moments in the cave?' she whispered.

Against her lips he murmured, 'I've not forgotten the rapture of your response. It was the passionate caress of a woman with an intense hunger for love. I accused you then of kissing somebody else—and now I know who that somebody was.'

Her arms clung to him with the desperation of a drowning person who feels the safe anchorage slipping away. 'You're wrong—you're absolutely wrong——'

Her words seemed to fall on deaf ears because he continued as though he hadn't heard her. 'And when we lay on your bed you revealed an inner longing—the yearning of one who was ready and willing to give everything. But suddenly you broke the spell. You drew back because I wasn't Ross Mitchell.'

She leaned against him, her head against his

shoulder, her arms about his waist. Frustrated, she searched in her mind for words that would convince him that Ross had *not* been uppermost in her thoughts, yet would *not* reveal that her longing had been for Adam himself. But somehow there just didn't seem to be any words.

He said, 'I suppose one of your main stumbling blocks is your own pride. I can understand you were deeply hurt when he chose your sister rather than yourself, but now he's ready to admit his mistake. Anyone can make a mistake.' His arms tightened about her and he kissed her again while she clung to him.

At last, looking up into his face she said with a touch of pathos, 'Adam—you don't understand.'

He rested his cheek against the top of her head. 'Of course I understand. You're a grand little person, Julie. I've become—quite fond of you.'

It was too much. Her patience gave way. She stepped back and stared up at him. '*Fond of me?* You've become quite *fond* of me? Is that all you can offer? Thank you for nothing. And as for making a mistake let me say that *you* are the world's expert——'

Further words died on her lips as car lights flashed along the drive. She waited for the vehicle to emerge from the trees, a vain hope simmering in her breast that perhaps it would not be Ross, but of course it was.

'Ah—your suitor has arrived,' Adam drawled with a faint hint of sarcasm edging his voice. 'See that you do the right thing.'

'Which is——?' she flashed at him.

But he made no reply.

The Rover pulled up beside the front steps and by the time Ross had stepped from it Julie had crossed the lawn towards him. A quick glance over her shoulder told her that Adam had discreetly vanished, and she couldn't help wondering whether he'd entered the house by a side door, or if he was still standing among the lilacs.

Ross's greeting was to snatch her to him. 'Julie—my darling—we're all set. Everything's fixed.'

She struggled angrily to slip from his grasp. 'What do you mean? What's fixed? We're all set for what——?'

'To become engaged, of course. I'm a free man. My engagement to Anna is off—finished—broken—anything you like to call it. And a damned good job too.'

'Is that a fact? How did it come about?' Despite herself she was curious. 'Was there a scene with loud wailings and tears? Or was it a more dignified affair—a formal breaking-off with Father at the head of proceedings?'

Ross leaned against the car and folded his arms with a self-satisfied air. 'Actually it was quite simple. I told Anna it would have to finish. I then called on your parents and laid my cards on the table. Anna was there too. I told them I couldn't cope with her excessive demands, and apart from that I admitted that you're the one I really love.'

'How touching. What did Anna way?'

'She shouted that you are more than welcome to me, or words to that effect. Your mother then confessed that she'd been worried about the engagement from the beginning.'

'What did Father say?'

'He ordered Anna to return the ring to me—despite the fact that I was breaking the engagement.'

'She returned it without any trouble?'

'Well—I picked it up from where she threw it. I then told your father I was coming to ask you to marry me. You know—he's an odd man, your father. He began talking about his will.'

She was nonplussed. 'His *will*? Are you sure?'

'You can bet your life I'm sure. He said that when he dies his entire estate will be sold and the money divided between his wife and daughters. He said that any neighbouring farmer who expected to enlarge his property through either of his daughters could think again. Don't you think that's lousy? Don't you consider he'd odd?'

'I think astute might be a better word.' She began to giggle.

Ross ignored her mirth. 'He then ordered your mother to bring a bowl of water so that he could wash his hands of the whole affair. She told him to go the bathroom and turn on the taps.'

Julie could visualize the scene. She laughed helplessly.

Ross fished in his pocket. 'Look—here's the ring. It's a beauty although I don't think Anna was over impressed by it.'

She looked at the cluster glistening in the moonlight. 'It's very nice,' she said without enthusiasm.

'Give me your hand. If it fitted Anna it should fit you. We're engaged now.'

She snatched her hand away. '*Like hell we are*—I'm sorry, Ross—I've no intention of marrying you. I've told you before——'

'But after all we've been to each other——'

'We were good friends and nothing more,' she told him patiently. 'I realise that now, very clearly indeed, and I want you to understand that it is a fact.'

'Listen, Julie——' He made a move to take her in his arms.

She skipped away from him, dodging his outstretched hands. 'Don't you dare touch me,' she snapped. 'Can't you get it into your head that I don't love you? I don't want you. Now would you please go. I can assure you there's no point in dragging out this discussion.'

'You're not giving me a chance,' he pleaded.

'There's no need. *I don't love you*—as I've already told you. I'll *never* marry you—and that's that.'

'I'll be damned if it is.' He peered at her through the moonlight, silent for a few moments as a new thought struck him. 'Don't try to tell me there's somebody else.'

She grasped at the suggestion. 'Of course there is. I thought you'd never guess.'

He gave a laugh that crackled with derision. 'Don't tell me you've fallen for this dashing Malvern fellow——'

'That's my business,' she shouted furiously. 'Now will you please go before he knows you're here and throws you off the place.'

'Ha-ha—you don't want him to know I'm here, eh? I'll be damned if I'll go before I've kissed you.'

She gave a cry as his hand grasped her arm and dragged her towards him. She felt his breath on her face, and as she fought and kicked against him she turned away to avoid his lips.

'You'll kiss me, Julie—you're damned well going to kiss me——'

She made futile efforts to push against his chest. 'No—no—leave me alone——' She began to sob with fury.

Adam's voice came from out of the shadows. It was low and tense with controlled temper. 'Are you too dumb to see the lady doesn't want you? Get your hands off her or I'll knock your blasted block off. Surely she's made the situation clear enough——'

Ross swung round, peering through the gloom to see where the voice had come from. He released Julie abruptly, causing her to fall to the ground, but the next instant Adam had lifted her to her feet.

Where had he been? she wondered. She hadn't seen him come down the front steps, therefore she presumed he must have remained standing in the shrubbery near the lilacs at the end of the drive. This meant he would have heard the entire conversation between Ross and herself, in which case he'd now understand she had no intention of marrying this man who had been her sister's fiancé.

It also meant that he would have heard her admit she loved somebody else—as well as Ross's accusation that she'd fallen for Adam himself. How would he take that statement? Would he believe it—disbelieve it—or simply ignore it? She would just have to wait and see what attitude he would take.

Humiliated by the whole episode, she became aware that the two men were arguing fiercely. Adam was ordering Ross from the property while Ross was stubbornly refusing to leave without her. The moonlight gave the scene an unreal atmosphere, making the two antagonists look like male performers in a play, and then, almost as if one cue, Elaine came on stage to resolve the situation.

Apparently a momentary lull in the sounds coming from the television had enabled her to hear angry voices in the garden. She left the room to investigate and now stood at the top of the veranda steps.

'Is there something wrong, Adam?' she called to him. 'Is it a matter for the police?'

'Yes—you can give them a ring. Tell them we have a trespasser on the place—one whose intention is burglary. Tell them to send a couple of husky fellows who are capable of handling an idiot.'

'I'll do that,' Elaine replied, then disappeared into the house.

It was enough for Ross. He leapt into the Rover, roared the engine and careered over the lawn as he turned the car.

Adam put his arms round Julie. 'Cling to me,' he commanded as he held her against him. 'It'll give him the message as he goes past. It seems it has to be drummed into him.'

It was not difficult to stand within the shelter of his arms, her head resting against his shoulder, and as the Rover's lights swept them with a brilliant glare he held her even closer.

'I trust that's the last you'll see of him,' Adam said as the hum of the car died on the night air.

Julie looked up at him. 'You heard everything?'

'The lot. I eavesdropped quite shamelessly from about twelve feet away. All I had to do was to get behind that snowball tree beside the end of the veranda and I had a box seat.'

She knew a sense of relief. 'I'm glad you heard it all.'

He gave a short laugh. 'I'm beginning to look upon your father with new respect. As you said, he's astute. And I like the bit about the bowl.'

'I wish you could meet Father,' Julie said. 'I'm sure you'd become friends. But never mind about him at the moment. Do you now believe that I'm *not* in love with Ross Mitchell and that I'll never marry him?'

'Yes. I'd say that point came across loud and clear— also the fact that you appear to be in love with somebody else. I hope you'll be happy with him— whoever he is. Now then—I'd better cancel that visit from the police.' He strode ahead of her, running up the front steps and leaving her alone in the moonlight.

Depression gripped her as she realised he'd simply brushed aside the fact that she could be in love with somebody else. It didn't matter in the least to him, and his casual attitude was like a deep wound from a knife. She wandered over to the lilacs, trying to recapture some of the earlier magic when he'd held her close to him, but somehow it had all disappeared.

Nor did she remain outside for long because the moonlight had taken on a cold eeriness which made her feel nervous. She also guessed she'd be questioned when she went inside, therefore she might as well get it over. And in this she was right. Both Lucy and Elaine were waiting for her.

'What was all that commotion about?' Elaine demanded.

'Didn't Adam tell you?' Julie hedged.

'He did not. He got in touch with the police and told them everything was under control. He then stamped off to his room and slammed the door. So—what was going on?'

Julie looked at Lucy. The soft brown eyes were curious although she hadn't asked any questions.

'I know you'll tell us when you're ready to do so,' the small woman said gently. 'I'll admit I am curious to know why the police should be called to cope with a man who visits you.'

'The police weren't really necessary,' Julie assured her, 'but the threat of them certainly persuaded him to go away.'

She knew she couldn't keep anything from Lucy, therefore she told her as much as was necessary about Ross Mitchell and his friendship with her sister and herself. 'He seems to have become very determined,' she went on ruefully. 'I'm afraid tonight's pestering from him won't be the last.'

'Your course is clear, dear,' Lucy said with conviction, her obvious hopes showing blatantly in her face. 'You must fall in love and marry someone else—someone like—like——'

Julie's laugh cut her short. 'Dear Lucy—that's a good idea.' How could she tell her she was already deeply in love with Adam—that she'd never known such gripping emotions, and that he was the only man in the world she wished to marry?

'You don't have to set your cap at anyone,' Elaine told her sharply and with a meaningful glare. 'If he broke off the engagement all you have to do is let him know that unless his harassment of you ceases, Anna will sue him for breach of promise. He'll think twice if he knows it'll hit his pocket.'

Julie was doubtful. 'My parents would never agree to that sort of publicity. Also—I doubt that it's ever done these days.'

'But he wouldn't know that. And if Anna's really demanding he's quite likely to believe it. It could give him a real fright,' Elaine speculated shrewdly.

'It'd give him a fright, all right, and at least it's worth a try. Thank you for the idea, Elaine.'

'Perhaps it'll help you to keep your sights away from Adam,' Elaine hissed in an undertone. 'We're almost engaged—do you understand? Lucy knows this but she won't admit it.' She sent a defiant glance in the small woman's direction but it was ignored.

Julie did not allow Elaine's statement to worry her, and she found she was able to laugh as the fear of Ross was suddenly swept from her mind. And although his face had been blotted from her thoughts while she carried on with Lucy's dresses, she was unable to erase the image of Adam which was constantly before her. It was also undermining to her self-esteem to know that at times he was in the next room—yet ignoring her.

She blinked at the tears that blurred her vision while working on Lucy's fourth dress. This was the floral with long sleeves, and although Lucy had been delighted with each one as it had been completed, this dress pleased her most of all. However, its progress did little to please Julie because she knew that its last stitches would mean there was no further reason for her to remain at Malvern.

These pretty florals have always suited me,' Lucy exlaimed happily as she surveyed herself in the long mirror.

Adam also admired it. He came into the room while Julie knelt to move a measuring stick round the hem. 'Very nice,' he said. 'It looks as if it could be finished in time for you to wear to the races tomorrow.'

Lucy stared at him with undisguised surprise. 'You mean you'll actually take me? How marvellous! I mean—it's been such a long time since I went to the races——'

Julie looked up and met his eyes. 'It'll be finished.'

He regarded her lazily. 'I'm sure you'll want to come with Lucy. Gallant's running and I notice Big Boy's been accepted for the same race. Naturally, you'll be shouting for your father's horse.'

She put in the last pin, then stood back to make sure the hem was straight. 'You're quite wrong,' she said without looking at him. 'I love Gallant, and I love Big

Boy, but I don't think I can bear to watch them fight it out together.'

He shrugged. 'They can only do their best.' There was a pause of several moments' silence then he surprised them both by saying, 'By the way—Elaine has just given me notice.'

Lucy gaped at him. 'Elaine is leaving us?'

'Yes. Her mother needs her at home. The shepherd and his wife who have been living in the house with Mrs Brady are finding it necessary to leave the district.'

Lucy's jaw dropped slightly, and although she waited for Adam to give more details he said nothing. At last she said, 'It's very sudden but—but I'm sure I'll manage the house.'

'You won't have to,' Adam assured her. 'I've arranged for Jack Cameron's wife to do part-time work here.' He turned to Julie. 'Would you help Lucy until Mrs Cameron takes up her job? She'd like to have a week with her sister before she settles into her new routine. It'll mean extending your stay here.'

'Of course I'll stay,' Julie assured him calmly. It was difficult to keep the eagerness from her voice, especially as she knew her colour had risen slightly. It was like a reprieve, and that night in bed she brushed away the feeling that her time at Malvern was drawing to an end.

The next day was fine and sunny for the races although its perfection was ruined by a strong wind which sent clouds scudding across the sky and stirred dust into whirlwinds. Adam drove Julie and Lucy to the meeting, and to say that he escorted them would be an exaggeration. He certainly took them in through the gates to the extensive grassy area which was covered with lines of parked cars, but there he left them.

As he stepped from the car he spoke to Julie. 'I'm sure I can rely on you to take care of Lucy.'

Lucy was indignant. 'Take care of me? Good gracious! I can take care of myself,' she snapped. 'Go on—off you go—we know you're just itching to get round to the horse stalls.'

He nodded to them briefly then disappeared among the crowds of people.

Julie felt vaguely disappointed when he left them, although she was well aware that horse-owners had more to worry about than the people they'd driven to the course. In any case she had her own duties to perform. She'd been asked to take care of Lucy.

Lucy was like an excited child, and as they left the car-park she looked about her with obvious pleasure. 'Raceday at Woodville always reminds me of a huge country picnic,' she said. 'People are causally dressed, and most of them eat their lunch sitting on the grass under the trees, or beside their cars. Now then—let's look at the horses before we go to the grandstand.'

They moved towards the stables where thoroughbreds were being attended by owners, trainers and stableboys. Some of the horses waited in stalls, while others were kept moving by being walked about the grounds. The wind blew manes and tails and flapped at dayrugs. They saw Adam, Ted and Tim busy with Gallant, but while Adam ignored them, Ted gave them a cherry wave.

'Molly's somewhere up on the stand,' he told them.

They moved away, Julie drawing Lucy towards her father's colt which she could see in the care of his trainer. 'That's Big Boy,' she said. 'He's not unlike Gallant. They're both large and dark.'

The trainer gave her a polite nod. 'Your parents and Anna are here,' he informed her. 'They're probably on the grandstand.'

Julie gave him a friendly smile and as they moved away she said to Lucy, 'I'd like you to meet Mother. I'm sure you'd get on very well together.'

Lucy sent her a shrewd look. 'And what about your father? Are you keen for Adam to meet him?'

'Yes—I'll be honest—it'd please me very much to see them become friends,' she admitted guardedly.

They moved across the grounds to look at the horses in the parade enclosure known as the birdcage, but as the wind was so blustery Julie decided it was time she persuaded Lucy to take a seat in the shelter offered by the stand which had its back to the strong south-westerly.

Dust swirled about their feet as they made their way across the tarseal towards the concrete steps. 'Dratted wind,' Lucy said crossly. 'It spoils everything, although the horses love it. Nor does it stop people from rushing to the tote. Just look at the queues in front of the windows.'

'Do you want to stand in line?' Julie asked with a laugh.

'No, thank you. I never bet on horses although I like to watch the races. And the jockeys are so colourful in their silks.'

'We're a fine pair to be associated with racehorses,' Julie admitted ruefully.

It was afternoon and just before the race in which Big Boy and Gallant were to compete, when Julie saw her mother, Molly and Anna on the stand. They waved to each other, and despite the crowd they were able to join forces and sit together.

'Where's Father?' Julie asked after her mother and sister had been introduced to Lucy. 'He'll miss the race if he's not here soon. The horses are in the birdcage.'

'Adam isn't to be seen either,' Lucy remarked anxiously. 'He always watches his horses run from the stand.'

Julie was more conscious of Adam's absence than she cared to admit. She turned her eyes to where the horses were being led round the enclosure before the stand, searching for the familiar colours. Tim was there, proudly wearing the Malvern green and gold, while the jockey mounted on Big Boy flashed her father's distinctive red and white diagonal striples. And as far as Julie was concerned there were only two horses in the race. Their coats glistened, their muscles rippled, and they both looked ready to go.

Claire Forysth gave an exclamation of relief. 'Ah—there's Walter. I was beginning to wonder if he'd get here in time to see the horses do their preliminary gallop.'

As Julie watched her father come up the concrete steps she also saw the man walking a short distance behind him. It was Adam. She noticed the strong wind flapping their trousers against their legs and she saw the dust twirling about her father's feet. If only they'd been walking together as friends instead of separately and as strangers, she thought.

And then she saw the whirlwind of dust spiralling upward. Her father made a wild snatch at his hat, and then he stood swaying, one hand held over his eyes while he groped blindly with the other to find a railing or support of some kind.

Adam was quick to move. He stepped forward and held Walter Forsyth's arm, and the next instant he was leading him down the steps and round the corner of the building.

Claire sprang to her feet. 'I'd better go to him.'

Julie laid a hand on her arm. 'Adam's with him, Mother. I'm sure he'll help him. What do you think could've happened? He was like a blind man.'

'I'm afraid it could be dust under his contact lenses. He's having trouble with them.'

'Why does he bother with them?' Molly demanded impatiently.

Claire laughed. 'You know Walter—and his vanity.'

Lucy said, 'Adam will have taken him to the nearest washbasin. I'm afraid they'll miss the race.'

This appeared to be more than probable. The horses had left the birdcage and had gone down the track for their preliminary gallop past the stand. They were then trotted up to the starting stalls where most of the jockeys dismounted until they were called into the places their horses had drawn. There was a short delay as one or two fractious animals gave trouble by refusing to enter the stalls, and during this time Julie watched anxiously for her father and Adam to reappear. How strange that Adam should've been the one to help Father, she thought.

At last the horses were all in and settled. The starter raised his hand, the gates were relased with a loud clang and the field of brightly coloured jackets flashed out into the public's view. There was a sharp sprint to get positions on the rails, and then they settled down to cover the length of the race.

The monotonous drone of the commentator's deadpan voice, so strangely lacking inflection, called the horses' positions as they thundered round the course. Naming half the field he told which ones were bunched together and which were straggling to the rear, but at last his voice quickened with interest, rising to an excited pitch as two horses drew ahead of the rest.

'Gallant and Big Boy have sorted themselves out and now lead the field neck and neck round the turn and into the straight—they're a couple of lengths clear of the field, it looks like a two-horse race, both jockeys have gone for the whip early in the frantic effort to hold the pace but now they're riding hands and heels—Big Boy pulls ahead but Gallant's caught him—Gallant's pulled ahead, Big Boy's beside him—stride for stride they're heading for the post. I can't separate them. It'll have to be the judge's decision, a photo finish will be called for——'

The crowd buzzed, arguing their opinions while they waited, and then the numbers went up to signify a dead heat.

During the race Julie lost control of herself as she stood up and yelled for Gallant. Then, when it was over, Claire smiled at her kindly and said, 'You had a small bet on Gallant, dear?'

Julie shook her head. 'No, I didn't put money on any of them.'

Her mother and Anna looked at her in shocked amazement, while Molly and Lucy sent each other a quick glance before they began laughing at something that appeared to amuse them.

'You shouted for Gallant!' Anna accused angrily. 'You *traitor*!'

Fortunately, before further argument could develop, they were joined by Walter Foysyth who was closely followed by Adam.

Claire was quick to show her sympathy. 'My dear—whatever happened to you? Although I think I can guess——'

But before he could reply Anna cut in angrily, 'Father—would you believe that Julie shouted like crazy for Gallant? Not for our own Big Boy, Father—but for *Gallant*.'

Julie said quickly, 'This is my father, Lucy. Father—this is Mrs Taylor.' She found it difficult to look at Adam although she knew his dark eyes were watching her.

As Walter shook hands with Lucy, Claire said, 'You haven't told us what happened. I was sorry you missed the race. It was quite exciting—a dead heat.'

Walter said, 'I didn't miss it, thanks to this young man. If it hadn't been for him I'd have been in real trouble. These damned contact lenses—I'm finished with them. My dear—I want you to meet Adam Malvern—my wife, Claire—and my daughter, Anna.'

Anna gaped at him, then her cheeks dimpled in their most attractive manner. 'Oh—so you're the—the Malvern man,' she said in a soft voice.

Her father glared at her, silencing her with a gesture. 'It was that confounded dust. When it got under my lenses I was completely helpless, but Adam took my arm and guided me to a basin in the gents' toilet where I could wash them. We got back to the rail just as the horses shot out of the starting stalls, so we didn't miss the race. It was damned good.'

Julie's eyes shone with gratitude as she gazed up at Adam. 'Thank you for helping Father,' she said quietly.

'Thank you for shouting for Gallant,' was all he said.

CHAPTER TEN

JULIE was secretly amused as she watched her father and Adam sitting side by side on the hard grandstand seat. Listening as they chatted amicably, her mind flicked back and a chuckle arose in her throat—a chuckle that had to be controlled, otherwise she'd have to explain her mirth, and that would be awkward.

What were the words Father had used when referring to that Malvern fellow who'd stolen his trainer? Arrogant—conceited—overbearing. And how had Adam referred to her father? He'd called him idiotic and self-satisfied—a man with a closed mind who refused to listen to explanations. They were two men who were antagonistic towards each other without ever having met, yet here they were, getting on like the proverbial house on fire.

The reason, she realised, lay in having something in common, their mutual interest being horses. The prominent sires and dams in Big Boy's pedigree were being proudly flaunted by Father, but by a strange coincidence some of them also featured in Gallant's bloodline. It was then realised the horses were related, and this fact was enough to draw the two men even closer. Suddenly they were like blood brothers with Adam issuing invitations for the Foysyths to have an evening meal at Malvern before driving home.

This suggestion was warmly seconded by Lucy who, Julie was delighted to note, was getting on very nicely with her mother. Their conversation centred round the sewing done by herself, and Lucy declared she'd be pleased for Claire to see it. Had Claire noticed the dress Molly was wearing?

They left as soon as the last race was over, Adam

driving ahead to guide the Forsyths to Malvern.

Julie, sitting in the back of the Peugeot, voiced her appreciation. 'Thank you for helping my father today, Adam, especially with that race just about to start. You could've so easily missed it.'

He met her eyes in the rear-vision mirror. 'Would you expect me to leave a man standing in a distressed state?'

'And it was kind of you to invite them for a meal,' she added.

'Might as well get to know them,' he remarked enigmatically.

'Why? I didn't think you'd be interested getting to know my parents, Father least of all——'

'Oh—well—when horse-owners get together they can't stop talking about their favourite subject,' he told her with a grin.

Lucy turned to smile at her. 'I'm so pleased to meet them, dear, and a meal is never any trouble when one knows there's plenty of food in the deep freeze.'

Julie knew that her parents would be interested in the old homestead and its gardens, and she noticed they were even more impressed by the Lindauer paintings hanging on the walls. Adam poured drinks, and while the men settled down to more thoroughbred discussion with their heads bent over the New Zealand studbook, Lucy took Claire on a tour of the house.

Julie and Anna went out to see Fay and her pups, and as they fondled each one in turn Anna sent her sister a sly look. 'You've got me to thank for all this—haven't you?'

Julie returned a pup to the straw and stroked Fay. 'What, exactly, do you mean?' she asked without looking at Anna.

'I mean this business of being able to stay here. If I hadn't stepped between you and Ross you wouldn't be here—would you? You'd be home—and perhaps engaged to him.'

'I suppose you're right,' Julie admitted reluctantly. 'To be honest I never really believed you were truly in love with him. Why did you deliberately come between us?'

A rebellious look crept into Anna's blue eyes. 'If you *must* know it was to see if I really could do it.' Then, as Julie stared at her incredulously, 'I suppose it's impossible for you to see what I've had to put up with.'

'What on earth are you talking about?'

'You've always been the pretty one—the one with the lovely face is how people are inclined to describe you. While you're around nobody looks at me—and it *makes me mad*. I knew you wanted to become engaged to Ross—it was sticking out a mile. So I decided to see if I could get him away from you, *and I did*. Can't you understand? It was a sort of truimph.' The words came tumbling out almost in the form of a confession.

'So—what has the exercise given you?' Julie asked quietly.

'Very little—apart from a small amount of satisfaction at the time—and even that's turned sour. I'm sorry, Julie. I know it made you unhappy. I'll never forget your face when Father said he'd given permission for Ross and me to become engaged.'

'You can forget it. Your triumph, as you call it, really did me a big favour. I'm no longer unhappy—at least not about that——'

'You're unhappy about something else?' Anna was interested.

Julie gave a short laugh. 'You're expecting me to confide in *you*? You've got to be joking.'

Anna looked at her thoughtfully. 'It's Adam Malvern, isn't it? You're in love with him.' Her voice took on an accusing note, as though seeing the situation clearly. 'You're in love with him but he won't look at you. So now you know how I feel when someone I fancy won't look at me. Now perhaps you'll understand the devilish feeling deep down inside that made me get to work on Ross.'

Julie ceased fondling Fay's silky ears. She stood up and said, 'I'm beginning to find this conversation most distasteful. Do you mind if we change the subject?'

'But you *are* in love with Adam,' Anna persisted. 'Go on—admit it. Don't you think I can tell——?'

Julie's face flamed. 'Mind your own damned business,' she snapped angrily. 'I'm going inside to see if I can help Elaine with the meal. You may stay with the pups if you wish.'

But when she entered the kitchen she found the meal well under control with savoury casserole and an apple pie already taken from the deep freeze. Her offer to assist with vegetables was brushed aside by Elaine who was in a disgruntled mood, the reason for this soon becoming clear.

'It's not fair,' she complained bitterly to Julie. 'I should *not* have to go home just because that shepherd and his wife have been dismissed. But Adam says he will not allow me to stay here while Mother is alone in the house. So the shepherd's dismissal from Mother's property means *my* dismissal from here. I tell you—*it's not fair.*' She stamped with such fury that Julie thought it wise to escape from the kitchen before Elaine's wrath was turned upon herself.

Later, Julie was almost relieved when her parents left for home because—for her—the evening held a few tensions. The meal passed pleasantly enough, and without any mention of Ross—for which she was thankful—but she was disturbed by the constant watchfulness that came from her mother and Anna. It was carefully concealed, but knowing them as well as she did she knew it was there and that they longed to ask outright if there was anything between Adam and herself.

Perhaps Lucy also sensed their curiosity because she said, 'I hope you don't want Julie to go home too soon.

She has promised to stay with me until Mary Cameron comes to take Elaine's place. Elaine leaves tomorrow, but Mary won't be here until she returns from visiting her sister. She's the wife of our farm manager and she'll come in each day to do the house.'

Claire's eyes were thoughtful. 'Of course we don't mind——'

'As far as I'm concerned she can stay forever,' Lucy smiled.

Adam turned and sent her an unexpected grin. 'Ah—but that's because you're planning your next winter's wardrobe,' he teased. He appeared to have been engrossed in a discussion about the many different breeds of sheep that were becoming popular in the country, but apparently the conversation between the women had not been lost upon him.

Julie felt a sudden apprehension. Had he also sensed the quiet observation that had been coming from Mother and Anna? Of course he had—he was so astute it would've been impossible for him to have missed it. The thought made her cringe with embarrassment. And was this why he'd almost completely ignored her during the meal and throughout the rest of the evening? Perhaps it was the beginning of an attitude with which he meant to continue.

During the next few days this appeared to be the case because, apart from rapid visits to the dining-room for meals, Julie hardly saw him. It seemed that he rushed in, sat down and ate, then disappeared.

Lucy also noticed his absence and began to make excuses for him. 'It's the time of the year,' she explained. 'They're shearing, you know, and there's a lot to be done. The shearing gang has to be kept supplied with sheep from early morning. Ewes and lambs have to be drafted, and at this time the lambs are usually drenched for worms. And when there are several mobs of ewes and lambs in the yards great care must be taken to see they're not mixed.'

Julie laughed. 'Dear Lucy—are you forgetting I'm a farmer's daughter? I know these things. I know all about the worry of the weather at shearing time because they don't shear wet sheep, and I know the shed must be left filled at night for the first run in the morning. I know Adam is busy,' she finished sadly.

'And there's another thing,' Lucy went on. 'The standard of shearing is always at its best when the boss is in the shed.'

Julie knew this also, yet she was unable to rid herself of the conviction that Adam was deliberately avoiding her. Well—there was nothing she could do about it except show him she didn't care—that she hadn't even noticed it. But she knew she did care—desperately. And she also knew that the moment Mary Cameron arrived there'd be no further excuse for her to remain at Malvern.

Days passed, shearing was over, and still Adam was seldom in the house. And then came a pleasant surprise when he looked across the table during one lunch hour and said, 'Would you like to come up to Whariti with me this afternoon? I'm bringing the two mares home. Dixie and Dell have been up there long enough.'

'Oh yes—thank you—I'd love to come.' She knew her face had beamed at the suggestion, but in case he guessed at her inner excitement that bubbled at the prospect of going out with him she said, 'Would Lucy like to come too?'

'She's welcome to come if she wants to.' He raised an eyebrow towards Lucy but did not press the point.

But Lucy had no desire to go up to Whariti. 'No thank you, dear,' she said to Julie. 'I'd prefer to get on the bed and have my rest. There's a cold wind blowing, so it'd be far too breezy for me. Make sure you put on a warm jacket, and you'd be wise to wear a head scarf or you hair will be blown away.'

'I don't need a scarf,' Julie assured her. 'Besides—I haven't got one with me here.'

'Then I'll lend you one,' Lucy declared with determination. 'You're sure to get out of the car and it'll give you that little bit of extra warmth.' She went to her room and returned with a square of blue nylon.

They left as soon as they'd disposed of the lunch dishes. Julie changed into a pair of jeans and put on a warm jacket. She folded the scarf into a triangle and dutifully tied the corners beneath her chin, finding that despite its light flimsiness it really did give extra warmth. It was difficult to stem the flow of excitement gushing through her veins, nor was it possible to control the glow in her cheeks, the sparkle in her eyes.

When she went outside the double horsetrailer had already been attached to the towbar of the Peugeot. Adam looked at her in silence until eventually he said, 'You look like a happy child going to her first party— or are you going to your first dance?'

She laughed joyfully. 'Actually, that's how I feel. I'm truly delighted to be going up to Whariti with you.'

He sent her a penetrating glance before turning to check the towbar. 'With me?' he asked without looking at her. 'What about this other fellow you've got in mind?'

She stared at him blankly. 'What other fellow? I don't understand what you mean.'

'Didn't I hear you tell Mitchell there's somebody else?'

She laughed. 'Oh—*that* fellow—for heaven's sake, I had to tell Ross *something* to convince him. Surely you understood——'

'I see. Well—let's get going.' He opened the car door for her.

They drove through a valley of farmlands, the metal road remaining flat until it began to wind upwards, hugging the hillside like a narrow grey ribbon. On their right the land fell abruptly to the lower levels of the valley, while on their left the overhanging growth of native shrubs and grasses brushed the side of the car and trailer. In places the graceful fronds of treeferns leaned over to shade the road as it twisted and turned against the contour of the hill.

At last it opened out to run through hilly farmlands. A farm homestead and its sheds were passed, and a short time later they ran along a narrow ridge where the land dropped steeply on either side. Julie peered down towards the depths on her side. 'What a horrible stretch,' she said. 'It's like a razorback.'

'Yes, but it's well fenced from the flatter land.' He then pointed ahead to where the two mares grazed in easier rolling country beyond the ridge. 'Look—there they are——'

A gateway into the field enabled him to turn the car in readiness for the homeward journey. They got out and she watched while he lowered the back of the trailer to form the ramp which would enable the mares to walk up into it.

She said, 'Can I help you catch them?'

He shook his head. 'There's no need. They'll both know I'll have oats in my pocket and they'll come to me at once.'

He was right. When he walked into the field the two mares came to meet him. Dixie's halter was slipped over her head and she was led back to be tied to the fence. Adam then took the second halter and went back to collect Dell.

While she waited for him Julie looked at the view which stretched away into a green tumble of haze-dimmed hills dotted by dark patches of scrub and pine or macrocarpa plantations. As Lucy had foreseen, a strong wind was blowing, forming waves in the long grass. A hawk riding against it drifted above her, and as she gazed upward to watch its effortless gliding a sudden sharp gust whipped the nylon scarf from her head.

It floated on the wind like a blue butterfly, causing her to rush into the field to follow its progress. On and on it went, never touching the ground until it came to rest near a clump of tussock on the far side of the fence. Lucy's scarf—she must get it. She scrambled through the wires and rushed at speed to snatch at it before the wind could lift it away to a further place.

But even as she almost had it within her grasp it was whisked beyond her reach, borne aloft on the breeze, then dropped again on the edge of an area where the land began to fall in a long sharp descent. Almost out of breath she raced after it, plunging forward to snatch at it with a gasp of relief, but as she did so she stumbled and fell—and the next moment she was tumbling, head over heels, bumping and rolling down the steep grade.

At times, completely out of control, she slid helplessly, and while one hand still clutched the scarf the other snatched at tufts of grass in a futile attempt to stop the fall which was suddenly brought to an abrupt halt as she crashed against a solid clump of scrubby growth. The breath had been knocked out of her, the world began to spin and she felt sick.

She lay still for several minutes, and as the feeling of nausea passed she wondered if she'd broken any bones; but when she moved her arms and legs one at a time she was relieved to find there was no real pain. The sun's rays caressed her, their heat intensified because the steep hill now protected her from the wind, and as she basked in the comforting warmth she decided to rest for a few mintues before making the effort of scrambling up the hill; therefore, staring at the sky and watching the passing cumulus clouds, she continued to lie still, feeling somewhat drowsy.

Adam's agitated voice shouting to her from above was the first sound that came to her ears. 'Don't try to move—just stay there—I'm coming down——' And sliding mainly on his seat he reached her within a few minutes. Kneeling beside her he gasped, 'Darling—what the hell——?'

She sighed wearily. 'It was Lucy's scarf. It danced along in the air like a balloon—or a big blue butterfly——'

His eyes became concerned. 'Did you bump your head? You're holding Lucy's scarf in your hand so what's all this about butterflies and balloons? Perhaps you gave your head a bang on the way down. Is it aching at all?'

'I don't know. Perhaps I did.' She closed her eyes as she tried to think clearly. For one mad moment she'd imagined he'd called her *darling*. Yes—perhaps she'd bumped her head. But his next words made her eyes fly open again.

'Darling—have you tried to move your arms and legs? Have you any pain at all—anywhere? Does anything really hurt?'

'I don't think anything's broken.' She looked at him wonderingly. 'You did it again. I wasn't sure the first time when you—you called me—darling.'

'That was careless of me. I've been trying not to do so for a long time. I'm afraid I lost control and it just slipped out.'

She stared at him incredulously. 'You mean—you've *wanted* to?'

'I knew that once I started I'd be lost. It's been difficult to hold out against you.'

'Not as difficult as it is for me to believe the words you've just uttered. Tell me—why did you hold out——?'

'Pride coupled with male ego, I suppose. I couldn't bear the thought of being rejected by you. At first I wasn't sure about your true feelings where Ross Mitchell was concerned, but I'd no sooner cleared my mind on that point when I heard mention of someone else. But all that was overriden when I saw you lying here from the top of the hill. I couldn't get down fast enough to make sure you were okay and to tell you I love you.'

Her eyes filled with tears as she gazed at him. 'Say that again—I didn't quite hear,' she whispered huskily.

'I love you, Julie. I've loved you for ages.'

'Since—since when?'

'Since the first time I kissed you in the cave, I think. It was like something exploding in my brain.' He lay beside her on the grass, his arms enfolding and holding her close to him as his lips found her own in a kiss that was like a dream come true. At last he murmured against her throat, 'Darling—tell me you love me. I'm longing to hear you say the words.'

'I love you, Adam,' she whispered shly. 'And that— that someone else I spoke of to Ross—was you. It's a wonder you didn't guess. Even he accused me of being in love with you.'

'I'm afraid I was too frothing-mad to think straight.'

'Poor Ross,' she said softly. 'Emotionally I don't think he's at all sure of himself. You told Elaine to tell the police he had burglary in mind, but you didn't really believe that—did you?'

'You can bet your life I believed it. He was there to steal my girl, wasn't he? Mighty determined about it, too.'

'But at that time I wasn't your girl.'

'You would've been the moment he'd left if I hadn't caught that remark about there being somebody else.'

She put her arms about his neck and clung to him. 'My dearest one, there'll never be anyone else.'

'We can be married soon?'

'You want to marry me? I don't recall being asked.'

'Can you doubt it? Please don't keep me waiting too long.' His embrace became fiercely urgent, his hands on her body possessive, drawing from her a small groan of ecstasy which he mistook for pain.

Loosening his hold at once he said, 'Darling—am I hurting you? I'm a thoughtless fool. I'm forgetting you've just had a nasty fall. Are you *sure* you're all right?'

She laughed a little shakily. 'I've probably got a few bruises, but perhaps it's time I stood up to make sure I'm all in one piece.'

He helped her to her feet and she trembled as she leaned against him, revelling in the comfort of his presence and in the pressure of the arms that held her close to him.

'You're shaking,' he said. 'Just stand still until this quivering fit passes. It's a nervous reaction.'

'S-so long as w-we d-don't slide further d-down the hill,' she said, her teeth chattering.

'It doesn't matter if we do because we're near the bottom. I'm still waiting to be told how this happened,' he reminded her.

'It was Lucy's scarf,' she explained against his chest. 'Th-the w-wind blew it away. It snatched it from my head and I chased it. I—I couldn't bear to lose Lucy's scarf.'

'She probably got a dozen of them.'

'That's not the point. She *lent* it to me and I intend to return it. I chased it until it landed where the hill started to fall abruptly, and then I stumbled and began to roll.'

'And a darned steep hill it is, too,' he said, looking up at the slope. 'It's really the end of that razorback stretch—the part where the land widens from the ridge and is still steep, but luckily not as perpendicular as below the ridge itself.'

'I was terrified. I thought I might be going down to a real drop and that perhaps you'd take ages to find me.' She followed his gaze as he looked upwards. 'The thought of struggling to the top again gives me the horrors.'

'You won't be doing that, my darling. We'll slide further down to where it's not so steep, and then we'll walk until we find an easier slope to climb. Do you feel like making the effort now, or would you rather wait for a while?'

She lifted her face to his. 'I'd like to stay here for a

long, long time because it's a place with a special significance for me—but I think we should go back to the horses. Besides—the longer I remain still the stiffer I'll become.'

'You're right. A hot bath is what you need.' He kissed her with long passionate caresses until he put her from him abruptly. 'Okay—let's go or I'll not be responsible,' he muttered huskily.

They slid most of the way down to the lower level where it was less difficult to walk, and then they made their way to a place where Adam scanned the slope above. 'Look—there are sheep tracks,' he said. 'We can follow their zigzag paths. Give me your hand.'

'It's yours.' She smiled happily at him.

He held her against him, again kissing her hungrily. 'Don't say things like that or we'll never get there,' he warned.

They started up the hill, moving from left to right along the narrow paths carved out by the sharp little hoofs of generations of sheep. By the time they reached the top he was almost dragging her, and they were both breathless.

'I'll not forget Whariti in a hurry,' she panted, gazing up at the peak where the television relay station pointed its finger.

'We're barely halfway up, but one day I'll take you to the top to see the vast panorama of rolling hills, mountains jutting up out of the land, and plains stretching away to a blue-grey haze of sea. But not today. At the moment I'm anxious to get you home.'

They found the two mares waiting patiently where Adam had left them safely tethered to the fence, and it took him only a short time to get them into the trailer. The homeward journey down the narrow metal hill road was taken at a slow and steady pace, and as they passed the razorback ridge Julie stared back to where a small clump of scrub had stopped her descent.

For the rest of the drive home she sat in a dream-like

daze, but when they reached the house she was jolted from this state by the sight of Ross Mitchell's Rover parked near the front door.

Dismayed, she said, 'Oh no—not again.' Then, sending an apprehensive glance towards Adam she tried to fathom his reaction, but he appeared to be quite unmoved.

He drove to the back of the house, then got out and opened the door for her. 'We'll see what he wants before we take the mares to their home paddock,' he told her quietly.

As they entered the back door Lucy came into the kitchen. 'It's that man again,' she whispered nervously. 'He *says* he's come to apologise for making such a fuss when he was last here, but I think he *really* wants to talk to Julie. I can tell he still refuses to believe it's all over between them——' She stopped suddenly as she looked at Julie's radiant face. 'Has—has anything happened——?'

Adam grinned. 'You can bet it has, Lucy. Julie and I are to be married—quite soon, I hope.'

Lucy clapped her hands with delight. 'Oh—my dears—I'm so pleased. I've been hoping and hoping it would happen.' She kissed Julie warmly, then hugged Adam.

He said, 'I'll go and deal with Mitchell.'

Lucy laid a hand on his arm. 'Wait—don't be too hard on him. He seems to be quite a nice man really, and you can't blame him for trying to win Julie. If you want to convince him that she's completely out of his reach you know the quickest way to do it.'

He paused as he was about to leave the room. 'I do? What, exactly, do you suggest? I've known you to come up with good ideas.'

'Have you forgotten your grandmother's ring? Your mother wore it and now it's Julie's turn. If she doesn't like it you can get her a different one, but somehow I think she'll value it.'

'By Jove—that'll give him the message. Why didn't I think of it? Lucy—you're a gem. Go and talk to him and we'll be there in a few minutes.'

'Actually—I've already given him a cup of tea,' Lucy confessed.

Adam took Julie's hand and led her into his bedroom. Holding her closely he said, 'We'll not be sleeping in here when we're married.'

'No?' Her colour rose as the thought of sleeping night after night with Adam sent tingles running up and down her spine.

'No. We'll sleep upstairs in the room my parents used. You've been in it, I suppose?'

'Yes, I've dusted it for Lucy. It's a large room with built-in furniture and its own bathroom. There are lovely views from windows that let in the winter sun. I never thought I'd be sleeping in it.' Her colour took on an ever deeper hue.

'It hasn't been slept in since my father died.' He became busy at a locked cabinet. 'You might not like this ring,' he warned. 'If you don't you must promise to say so and I'll get you something different. You'll tell me——?'

She nodded, visualising a wide gold band of antique design, probably with small stones such as rubies or garnets so deeply set they could hardly be seen. At the same time she knew it didn't matter what it was like. She knew she would love it because it was the ring Adam was about to put on her finger, and despite its age, style or appearance, it would be her engagement ring. Nor would anything make her change it.

He turned to her with a small box which he flicked open to reveal a ring so different from the one she'd conjured up in her mind she could only gape at it in silence. It was a bar of five large diamonds.

'If you don't like it——' he began.

'What on earth makes you think I might not like it?'

she asked wonderingly. 'I don't know when I've seen a more beautiful ring.'

'It's rather opulent, but I'd like you to wear it. My mother was very proud of it. I believe my grandfather bought it in Holland.' He slipped it on her finger where it sat comfortably, then he took her in his arms where she relaxed like a contented child. 'I can't live without you, darling,' he murmured against her lips, 'but I suppose we'd better get this other business over and be done with it.'

When they went into the lounge Julie kept her hands in the deep pockets of the jacket she was still wearing. Ross stood up as she entered the room, and, ignoring Adam, he went towards her. His voice was low as he spoke to her.

'Julie—my dearest—you know why I've come. I had to tell you I'm sorry about the way I behaved last time I was here. You do understand I was upset?'

'Yes. There's no need to worry. I've forgotten about it.'

'Good.' He was suddenly full of confidence. 'I want to talk to you in private. There are two things I want to tell you, so perhaps we could go somewhere away from listening ears.'

She shook her head. 'There's nothing that can't be said in front of Lucy—or Adam. We'll stay in this room.'

Ross sent a glance of appeal towards Adam who leaned nonchalantly against the mantelpiece, and then towards Lucy who sat upright in an armchair. Then, as neither of them appeared to have the slightest intention of leaving the room, he gave a resigned shrug and said, 'Very well—it doesn't matter if they know I don't believe a word of what you said when you told me there was somebody else. I've been thinking it over and I've realised you were simply fobbing me off to give yourself time——'

'No Ross, you're quite wrong,' Julie cut in. She

looked at him steadily. 'There definitely is somebody
else. Adam and I are to be married. I love him very
much.'

His expression became mocking as he gave a short
laugh. 'Malvern? Huh! You're merely trying to fob me
off again.'

Lucy became impatient. 'Young man—why can't you
take no for an answer? Why do you persist in thinking
of yourself rather than of Julie's happiness?'

He sent Lucy a lofty smile. 'Because I don't
believe——'

The words died on his lips as Julie took her left hand
from her pocket and held it towards him. He opened his
mouth to speak, then shut it again as the flash of fiery
brilliance caught and held his gaze. He swallowed twice,
but still remained silent.

Julie smiled inwardly. She knew that Ross, who had
recently become acquainted with the value of diamond
rings, was suitably impressed. 'I'm sorry, Ross,' was all
she could say.

Adam drawled lazily, 'We can only hope you're
convinced at last, Mitchell. Julie and I are to be married
as soon as the wedding can be arranged. But didn't you
say there were *two* things you wished to tell her?' His
voice was mildly curious.

'Yes. The second matter really depended upon what
Julie had to say to me today. I've had an offer for my
farm which I might as well accept. I'll probably go
down to the South Island. You won't see me again,
Julie. I can only hope you'll be very happy.' He then
surprised them by turning to Adam and holding out his
hand. 'As for you—congratulations. I suppose it's a
case of the best man having won.'

'I'll drink to that,' Adam replied with a grin. 'How
about something a little stronger than tea? Would you
like a Scotch?'

'Thanks—I could do with one,' Ross replied gruffly.

Adam poured whisky for Ross and himself, and

sherries for Lucy and Julie, and a short time later Ross
left, departing out of Julie's life forever.

As the Rover disappeared along the drive Adam told
Lucy about Julie's fall down the steep hillside. 'A hot
bath with some of your magic mix is what she needs. I'll
turn on the taps.' He disappeared towards the
downstairs bathroom.

'Magic mix——?' Julie's eyes held a question.

Lucy smiled. 'It's a recipe I found in an old treasury
of secrets. It's a mixture of Epsom salts, eucalyptus oil,
menthol solution, iodine and a water softener. It makes
a homemade mineral bath that soaks away tension,
tiredness, aches and pains, and you must lie in it for
fifteen minutes.'

It was indeed a magic mix because later she stepped
from the warm water without a single ache, and
wondering if the hillside fall had been a dream.

But the heavenly bliss of knowing Adam loved her
was anything but a dream, and later, when the moon
hung in the night sky like a silver crescent, he led her
out into the garden. Spring had given way to summer,
the roses were in bloom, and as they paused to drink in
the heady perfume rising from the masses of pink, red
and yellow blossoms he said reminiscently, 'Mother
always had roses in a large silver bowl in the lounge.'

She made a mental note to find the bowl and fill it.
Then, turning, she looked back at the house and was
surprised to find it ablaze with lights. The upstairs
windows glowed behind the balcony stretching across
the front, and downstairs they threw oblongs of light
across the drive and on to the lawn. She looked at him,
searching his face for an explanation.

He gave a small self-conscious laugh, then held her
close to him as he said, 'When we came out I asked
Lucy to turn on every light. The old house, all lit up
inside, is telling you how it feels—and how I feel. It's
giving you its own special welcome. Before you came it
was dead—and so was I. But now the old home and I

are taking on a new lease of life. My darling—I can't tell you how much I love you. I can only try to show you during the years we'll share together.'

She sighed contentedly, nestling within the shelter of his arms as they held her against him.

For the millions who can't read
Give the Gift of Literacy

One out of five adults in North America
cannot read or write well enough
to fill out a job application
or understand the directions on a bottle of medicine.

**You can change all this by joining the fight
against illiteracy.**

For more information write to:
Contact, Box 81826, Lincoln, Neb. 68501
In the United States, call toll free: 1-800-228-8813

**The only degree you need
is a degree of caring**

Six exciting series for you every month... from Harlequin

Harlequin Romance
The series that started it all

Tender, captivating and heartwarming...
love stories that sweep you off to faraway places
and delight you with the magic of love.

Harlequin Presents

Powerful contemporary love stories...as individual as the women who read them

The No. 1 romance series...
exciting love stories for you, the woman of today...
a rare blend of passion and dramatic realism.

Harlequin Superromance®
It's more than romance...
it's Harlequin Superromance

A sophisticated, contemporary romance-fiction
series, providing you with a longer,
more involving read...a richer mix of complex plots,
realism and adventure.

Harlequin American Romance™
Harlequin celebrates the American woman...

...by offering you romance stories written about American women, by American women for American women. This series offers you contemporary romances uniquely North American in flavor and appeal.

◆

Harlequin Temptation™
Passionate stories for today's woman

An exciting series of sensual, mature stories of love...dilemmas, choices, resolutions... all contemporary issues dealt with in a true-to-life fashion by some of your favorite authors.

◆

Harlequin Intrigue
Because romance can be quite an adventure

Harlequin Intrigue, an innovative series that blends the romance you expect... with the unexpected. Each story has an added element of intrigue that provides a new twist to the Harlequin tradition of romance excellence.

Harlequin Books·

PROD-A-2

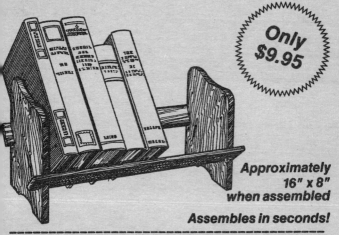